Shadow By My Fireplace

Harper M. Tremblay

Cover Design by Anne Hessel

For those readers who find comfort within the pages of Shadow's story, whatever your reason may be, know that I am right alongside you. Shadow's story is uncomfortable at times, but where one person may find a deep discomfort, another may feel heard for the first time. To that end, I would make one thousand people uncomfortable so one person feels that some part of their story is told.

Also, to the Great Lakes, may your legends ever live on.

Also by Harper M. Tremblay

The Dark Side of the Sun

Contents

A Note About Content

This story contains the following content:

- Sexual assault
- Torture
- Human trafficking
- Captivity, dehumanization, conditioning
- Suicide attempt (unsuccessful)
- Nonconsensual drugging, opiates, addiction, drug overdoses
- Foster system-related trauma
- Character death
- PTSD
- Recovery from trauma
- Happy ending

If this book isn't for you, no worries! But if it is, we hope you enjoy this story about survival and healing ...

Chapter 1

When Sacha was a child, he sometimes heard a story from his mother about a mighty knight who fished a powerful witch out of the waters with nothing more than goldenrod. Brought down to his knees by his enemy, the knight had no choice but to summon her. She took pity upon the knight and blessed him with gifts and healing so he might ride into the horizon.

Even if knights were of the bygone past, Sacha still found himself wishing to be one as a child.

Those days seemed so far away, even if they were the only comfort he had within the walls built by his captor. He'd been so hopeful back then. When did hope begin to feel like a stranger and misery a friend? Where were those lofty dreams he had back then? Why couldn't he imagine himself inhabiting that skin again?

Darkness encased the room, reminding Sacha how deep in the belly of the beast he was. It was slightly damp, too, but dampness was better than dry air. Dry air would hurt his fresh wounds more. There wasn't so much as a blanket or a roll of bandages for the oozing, burning gashes on his back. They were surely infected, but the merciful embrace of death was preferable to a life like his.

The skin he inhabited now was one of a doll, a pet for a corrupt, wealthy man. He could never be anything more.

Yes, Sacha was to be out of sight, out of mind when he wasn't wanted by Master. Nobody could know that he existed. Nobody could know what Master was involved with. He needed to be hidden away from the world, away from the light, away from the prying eyes that surely followed Master wherever he went.

Tears formed in Sacha's eyes. What he wouldn't give for a warm embrace or even just a blanket. He was naked, bleeding, and filthy on the floor. Of course he was freezing. He was many days into starvation, many days into blood loss.

Was the end coming soon?

Master hadn't been down to see him in days. The noises upstairs were almost non-existent since yesterday.

Maybe Master was leaving him there to die. Yet Sacha knew that to be too merciful a fate.

A rush of chills startled him. Yes, the wounds *were* in fact infected. A wave of nausea washed over him next. He was seldom nauseous. It wasn't a good sign.

Maybe he's waiting for me to try to escape.

Chills tore through his flesh again, brought on by the memory of his last escape attempt rather than the fever.

Sacha wasn't sure he remembered what it was called, but Master said that Sacha would never walk again after the impending punishment.

A simple mercy, perhaps. The less he could do, the less he would upset Master.

Maybe the festering wound would infect his blood and give him the ultimate relief.

Sacha decided. He would go upstairs.

The door to his room was unlocked. That wasn't normal. Master was testing him.

He opened the door all the way to see an empty house.

With featherlight steps, Sacha walked to the front door. The last time he'd left the house, he'd come back cold and dripping wet after being left outside for countless hours with broken ankles and tied to a tree. The next week, he'd developed Lyme. It was one of the few times that Master had ever bought him pills – antibiotics.

Sacha took a deep breath. Escape was what Master wanted him to do, after all.

Legs shaking, Sacha pushed the front door open to the wilderness, the same wilderness he was entirely unfamiliar with, yet felt like an old friend. He didn't look back as he ran, a deer in the hunt. Eyes closed, he pushed forward, pushed forward, ran through the underbrush, until he no longer recognized anything and the forest was all the same.

Soon enough, those scarred, damaged feet couldn't hold him up anyone. Not with the weight of infection in his bones. He realized that the adrenaline had carried him far away from home.

Maybe I'll die here.

A bird twittered a bit overhead as he collapsed, finally too weak to ever lift himself up again.

It wasn't exactly a bad place to die. At least it wasn't in Master's home.

As the void of unconsciousness swallowed him, Sacha took a deep, peaceful breath. It wasn't a bad day, not at all.

***

Cyril was quick to gather his materials for the day. Although town wasn't too far away, he tired far too quickly of the crowds to find himself there long enough to finish shopping. He preferred his upcoming once-yearly trip to pick up seeds and iron for his gardening to interacting with anyone, ever.

He was early to rise, early in the sack. After all, the best picking times for his fruits and vegetables was early in the morning, just after the dew but before the scorching sun of high noon.

Of course, that was often the best time for hunting, too, when the deer were still out. The fruits and vegetables always took priority. He could easily freeze deer meat, while fruits needed to be picked within a very tight window to taste their best.

Despite having some beets ready to pick, he chose the hunt that day. The meat from his last catch was gone and the winds were turning cold. He needed all the pelts he could get to avoid having to buy blankets. Plus the meat – hunting any doe in the winter was a silly idea, what with their bellies full of babies. He needed to store as much meat as possible before the cold came.

Deer, he would not find that day.

After he gathered all his supplies and he went towards his usual trapping spots, he stumbled across something he'd never expected to see.

A man laid in front of him, beaten bloody and covered in horribly infected wounds. Instincts from a time long before his quiet cabin in the woods took over as he approached the man, shouting at him, shaking him, begging for him to be alive.

The scene was familiar, far too much so. He pressed his finger to the man's neck, feeling for his pulse. It was shallow and fast. More worryingly, the man's skin was also burning to the touch.

Cyril didn't realize there was tension in his shoulders until they began to hurt. He took a few moments to slow his breathing.

He probably isn't contagious. The fever's from all those wounds.

That was probably a worse case than if it *was* contagious. If he was sick from the wounds, the infection might be in his bloodstream.

Shit.

Cyril dropped his hunting gear, those protective instincts quickly taking over. He picked the man up in his arms and rushed back to his cabin.

Beyond the panic, Cyril was unmistakably angry. He hated people. As he laid the man on his bed without care for the bloody, dirty mess that was his body and got a thin sheet to cover him, it was easy to remember why.

No, he didn't hate the survivors of tragedy. He hated all the wretched people that wrought people into stories. Memory told him well that he was just as capable as the next person of perpetuating such tragedies. If he couldn't trust himself, Cyril certainly couldn't trust anyone else.

He hurried over to the tap. The water would be cold, easier to cool with ice. Cyril poured some water into the bowl, then took some ice from the freezer. Quietly, he dipped a rag in the ice water, wrung it, and put it on the man's forehead.

Bitter panic rose in Cyril's chest when the man made not a sound in response to the cold compress.

Would the beaten stranger really die in his house?

Another one I couldn't save.

The idea was unbearable.

He wouldn't let it happen again. He couldn't. He couldn't live with himself if he did. Cyril was tired of letting people go, stranger, friend, foe, or family.

I'll save this one if it's the last thing I do.

Cyril pulled the skin up on the man's arm. It held up perfectly and only went back down when Cyril pressed again.

I still have supplies, right?

Without another thought, Cyril went to the cabinet he dared not touch. Inside was a collection of vials, needles, tubing, and instruments – all from that other time in his life. Quietly, he picked out a bag of saline and some tubing. He didn't have an IV pole. He'd long gotten rid of the thing. He *did* have a bedpost and tape. It would have to do.

To his surprise, the skin prepper in his IV kit was still functional. Placing a needle came as easily as breathing. Blood was very, very slow to come up, but he knew he had a good vein when he pulled the plunger on his IV flush back.

A good vein had been surprisingly easy to find on the dehydrated man. He only had one more bag of fluids, but if the IV fluids got the man to wake up, Cyril could give him water.

Once the drip was going on the IV, Cyril went back into the vials, looking for anything, any antibiotic he might have. The man needed them desperately, and he wouldn't have time to reach the pharmacy in town before it was too late.

To his absolute relief, he found a one-year-expired vial of cefepime. Cyril found it a blessing to have anything at all, much less something he would administer if given the choice.

Quickly, he drew up the man's dose and put the bottle back. With the speed he was used to having back in his emergency room days, Cyril injected the medicine into the man's IV, allowing himself to breathe a small sigh of relief.

Next, he dipped the rag on his forehead back into the ice water. How long had it taken the cloth to feel fresh out of a warmer?

I need to check him for ticks.

Cyril lifted the sheet from the oozing, bloody wounds covering the man's body. He noticed something he hadn't before around the man's neck – *a collar.*

Cyril swallowed.

There were tattoos on him, too. He could only assume they weren't given of his own will.

Fuck.

By some miracle, the man did not have a single tick anywhere on his body. Further investigation of the man's body had Cyril saying his prayers.

Cyril concluded that if the man survived, that would be the real miracle.

The wounds on the man's legs came first. He'd need to compress them. The man would be laying down for far too long. Blood clots were always a concern, especially with so much broken flesh.

With a bottle of hydrogen peroxide, cotton balls, and bandages, Cyril started to work on the torn up flesh that comprised the man's legs.

This part, he was less familiar with. He had always had help in these situations. Scrubbing each of the wounds so carefully and so deeply was tiring.

Cyril thought back to that time, three years ago, before his peaceful little life in his cabin in the woods.

Well, not so peaceful now, I guess.

He found himself lost in his thoughts for a long time. Familiar faces of people he'd saved and, more noticeably, the ones he didn't, flashed through his mind as he worked away at the wounds, covering them and cleaning them.

Even if some part of him found relief, perhaps even gratification, in healing, it was easy to remember why he'd abandoned medicine for the life he had now. People were undeniably cruel creatures.

Suddenly, the collar was bothering him. Cyril pulled a knife out of his boot and, with the utmost care, cut the leather off of the man's neck. Under it, he saw burns. With disgust, he looked back at the collar and noticed the prongs.

Fucking shock collar.

It took everything in him to steady himself again.

Although he knew it wasn't healthy, he found himself focusing on the sad memories of his life before to steady himself. Sorrow was easier to control than ire.

He was like that until he looked up from his work and saw scared, pale brown eyes looking up at him. Suddenly, the world froze.

He's alive.

CHAPTER 2

Upon seeing those eyes, Cyril was immediately met with a problem he hadn't yet thought of: what exactly was he supposed to say to the man?

He didn't have much time before the man began to whimper and attempt to stand. Of course, he was weak. Cyril immediately jumped to get the man back in bed and to try to prevent him from standing again.

"You're very injured. There's a chance you've gone septic. Please, just rest."

When Cyril looked down at the man, he was huddling and covering his face, whimpering. It was almost as if he was saying. "Don't hurt me."

The fear on the man's face gave him pause. He tried to remember what he said to all those terrified people back then, but failed to bring up even a semblance of what exactly he used to say. Could he really tell the man that everything was going to be fine? He doubted that the man would believe him.

In all honesty, he didn't even know that he could promise the man that everything was going to be fine. All he could do was hope – hope that the man wasn't really septic and hope that the injuries would heal well.

More than anything, Cyril wanted to know what happened to the man. He understood that the man was probably delirious, if not from the fever then from the pain.

"Who did this to you?"

The man froze. Terror filled his eyes. His breathing began to grow deeper and faster. Soon enough, he was having a full-blown panic attack.

Cyril grabbed the man's shoulders, but the man immediately, with his whole body, flinched away. Cyril quickly let go, trying to figure out what to do next.

He went to the kitchen, only to find the man trying to get up from his bed again. Cyril ran back over and put him back down in the bed.

"You need to stay lying down." Cyril made sure to use a stern tone, but not too stern. He didn't want to make the panic attack worse.

The man looked at him with that quickly familiar look of terror, but listened. Somehow, Cyril felt awful. The man looked so dejected and afraid as he went back to the kitchen in search of something that he could use to ground himself. Cyril decided on some ice and brought it back to the man.

Again, the man looked at him with the fear one would have for an angry god. The look made Cyril sick to his stomach.

It finally occurred to Cyril that the man was probably kept as some sort of pet or plaything judging by the collar that had been around his neck. That thought made him feel even more ill.

"Here. Put this in your mouth." He put the piece of ice in the man's hand. "No tricks. Focus on the cold. I – " Cyril took a deep breath. "It was wrong to ask you such a personal question right off the bat. I can't promise that you'll be okay, but I'll do everything in my power to make you feel better and get through this."

A look of distrust flashed across the man's face. Terror was quick to replace it. The man obediently took the ice and flinched a bit when it hit his mouth. He shrank away from Cyril. Cyril simply let it happen while the man calmed down.

"Can you tell me your name?"

The man froze.

Cyril took that as a negative.

"It's okay. I won't be upset with you."

He hated how easily those words came to him again. He hated the memories and instinct that seemed to be quickly taking over.

Still, the man remained deathly quiet. Cyril might have mistaken the small twitch of his head as a shake to tell him no if he wasn't paying so close attention to the man's other body language.

What exactly was he meant to do with someone who couldn't speak?

"Could you write your name?"

Again, the terrified silence quickly filled the room. Frustration grew in Cyril. Normally, he had other people to help him.

The colors of the orange sunrise were enveloping the walls with their warmth. Cyril needed to hunt. He needed to tend to his garden. However, he also needed to help the man. That overwhelmed any need to take care of himself. Cyril certainly wasn't going to look for help, either.

He forced himself to take a deep breath. "Well, I hope that eventually you will be able to. I'm sure you're in a lot of pain right now. I'm sorry that I don't have better painkillers. Just this salve. We'll go slowly, okay?"

No response from the man. Cyril held back a sigh as he continued his work on the man's legs.

***

The man finally left Sacha alone after agonizing, horrible hours of the man trying to talk to him while tending to his wounds. Sacha had half a mind to pay attention to those words like a running stream, something meant to calm him, but only made him crave something he couldn't have.

Surely, the man had to be one of Master's friends, living so far out. Surely, he knew who Sacha was.

Something made Sacha doubt that. Whether it was the needle in his arm with the drip of water – sweet, precious water only given out on Master's commands – or the way he applied that salve that took his pain away, Sacha wasn't sure.

Oh, the salve. The salve worked mercifully quickly. Though the man apologized time and time again for it hurting, Sacha couldn't help himself. He simply melted into the man's touch. When he started crying, the man was concerned and confused, but he simply didn't understand.

You're simply made for this.

You're beautiful when you're hurt.

Look at you, hurting so beautifully in silence. I couldn't have wished for a better pet, could I?

Sacha heard that horrible chuckle in his ears with every tear he shed. He felt the way that Master had grabbed his hair, pulling it so painfully tight that he wanted to whimper, but couldn't. Not in front of Master.

Those are lovely, silent tears, my dear. Are you sure you don't need more medicine?

No, the man who was applying the salve didn't understand. Sacha was made for pain. He was made to serve. It was his job to be silent through it all. If he made a sound, he'd be given that horrible medicine again. He would hardly be able to move.

So, Sacha forced himself to be numb. He applied ice to the pulsating, hot, angry wounds in his heart. He pinched the veins and arteries near his heart to distract from the pain. He forced himself to remember the pain of each lash of his last punishment. That would be his fate again if he didn't obey.

He needed to be good for when Master would come again. The man would tell Master everything he'd done. He'd tell Master if he said anything.

I can't have the medicine. Not again. I don't want to take it again.

Snap.

Snap.

Snap. Snap. Snap.

Bzzt.

White-hot fear filled Sacha's veins. His vision went out of focus, then came back sharper than ever. His breathing went shallow. His muscles tensed.

On shaky, weak legs, Sacha hurried up from the bed. The man wasn't around to put him back down. Sacha took a few tentative steps, but yelped in pain at a horrible twinge in his side. He went crashing to the ground the next moment.

The man rushed into the room.

He looked down and saw the crumpled, pathetic mess on his floor. Sacha could almost feel the scorn in his eyes. He was so, so stupid. He'd made a noise. The man was going to drug him now. He was going to be punished.

"You need to stop getting up."

The tone in the man's voice made his heart drop.

The man picked him up. It wasn't a difficult feat. Food was a luxury and water was a gift. Sacha didn't weigh what he used to.

"Stay in bed."

Sacha wanted to shake his head. He didn't deserve to continue lying in bed. He was an awful pet. He needed to be on the floor, where he belonged.

"I'm serious. You need to rest."

The man sighed. Sacha flinched a little.

He felt something cold above his head. Again, Sacha flinched away.

"Stay still. It's just a cold cloth for your fever."

Sacha listened eagerly. He wanted to avoid punishment for the noise he'd made.

Why wasn't the cloth going in his mouth again?

He had a fever?

He almost always had a fever.

Surely, the man knew that. He knew it was normal for Sacha to have a fever.

"I'm making soup. No electrocution. No shock collar. I'm starting the element."

How does he know?

"I'll be back soon."

Sacha didn't realize he'd been holding his breath until the man left the room. Finally, he could breathe again. He didn't want to make noise.

Soon enough, the man came back with a bowl in hand.

"I'm going to feed you, if that's okay." He looked down at the bowl. "This is just puree soup. It should go down easily. You can only have a little because you're extremely thin. I don't want the food to hurt you if you haven't eaten in a while."

Sacha wanted to nod. It made sense. He was only deserving of what the man decided he was deserving of. Anything more would make him look human.

"Okay, let's do this. We can do this."

Sacha wasn't sure if the man was saying that to him or to himself. He wasn't deserving of the answer.

The first spoonful had a texture that made Sacha want to grimace. However, he was too scared of being force-fed the food to ever let his fear show.

Spoonful by gentle spoonful, the man fed Sacha carefully. When he was done with the small bowl of soup, he praised Sacha.

"You did a good job."

Somehow, the praise felt hollow. It wasn't from Master, so it didn't matter. Master was his world. Master was everything.

"I – " The man set the bowl aside. "I didn't introduce myself. My name is Cyril Galanos. I live alone out here." He looked away from Sacha and out the window. "Whoever kept you, I'm not related to them. I won't do anything to harm you. I hate people who do shit like this. You ... you don't have to fear me, okay? I know that's probably hard right now. But I promise I won't hurt you. Just ... try to believe it. Even for a little bit. It'll help both of us."

Sacha pretended that he could believe those words, but he knew them to be blatant lies. After all, this had to be a test. It had to be a trick set up by Master to test his loyalty.

"I need to get some things done, but I'll be back to check on you later. Please, rest. Don't leave this bed. If you pull that needle out trying to get up, it'll hurt a lot."

Perfect. If he needed pain, he knew how to get it.

He pretended to understand, like he pretended to believe the man ... Cyril.

It was only a matter of time, after all. Master would find him again. Just like he'd promised. If he didn't die before then, he'd be forced back into an unimaginable hell.

Somehow, death seemed more appealing. Cyril must have known that. Why else would he save him?

CHAPTER 3

When had Sacha first learned fear?

Of course, everyone thinks they know fear. It's only natural to believe that fearing spiders or snakes or getting sick is knowing fear.

Sacha begged to differ.

He hadn't known fear, not really, before he met Master.

At first, he didn't know Master's power. He knew that Master was powerful in the traditional sense – he had a lot of money and connections all over the world. But that wasn't the true power that Master had. No, his true power was something much more terrifying.

He could control the mind.

He could bend it to his will and make someone do whatever he wanted, one way or another.

It was coming back to Sacha now, the day that he learned fear. He'd tried to escape, hadn't he? He'd tried to fight back in some small way.

Oh, Master had been furious. He looked like an angry bull, ready to charge. Perhaps not a prey animal – that was Sacha. Master was closer to an angry lion that day, ready to claw apart whatever had infringed on his pride.

The needle had taken only an instant to find purchase in Sacha's skin. He didn't feel it immediately, but the medication was quick to take effect. He didn't feel anything but an overwhelming anxiety. He wanted to rip his skin off.

However, there was an unmistakable heaviness in his limbs. When he tried to stand, he found himself so dizzy that he couldn't move. Master ended up needing to carry him. Within minutes, his vision was blurry. He couldn't see a damn thing.

His heart was beating so quickly that it brought on a panic that just couldn't come through. He felt like screaming, but every bone in his body was too tired to even let out a noise.

Sacha spent a day, alone, in the basement, riding wave after wave of panic about events that never came to pass. He hated it. He wanted to tear his clothes apart and find new ones. He wanted to run a marathon and never look back. More than anything, he wanted to let tears out. He *wanted* to have a panic attack – let it be done and over with instead of the constant prolonging.

How his heart sank when he saw Master with a preloaded syringe the next day.

"Please. Please. Please. Please. Don't. Don't do that to me again. I can't take it."

Back then, Sacha thought that a human plea would get through to the monster in front of him. He thought he wouldn't be given the medicine again.

"Why, Sacha? Tell me why," Master cooed. "Why shouldn't I continue your punishment when you explicitly went against my rules?"

"It's unbearable." Sacha had not even the strength to stand and meet Master. "I'll take anything else instead."

"Anything else, you say?" Master had a wicked smile on his face.

"*Anything.*"

"Well, then." Master threw the needle in the bucket where Sacha used the toilet most days. "Let's make sure you don't use those feet again for a while, hmm?"

Sacha's eyes went wide as Master took his foot in his hand. As he pulled his ankle at a terrible angle, Sacha found himself wanting to scream, but not having enough air in his lungs to make anything above a whisper. Master smiled at his silence while a giant *crack* filled the room.

"I like you like this." He took the other foot and repeated the same action. Sacha wanted to cry. He wanted to scream. He wanted to fight but the pain in his ankles was so, so bad. "We'll do this again."

From that day forward, when Sacha saw a needle, he couldn't help but be overwhelmed with that true fear he'd learned from Master.

Those twenty-four hours had taught him true fear.

***

Cyril knew something was wrong with the man when he got back from his hunt. It was an instinct he'd developed years ago that watched the shaking, sweating mess on his bed and knew something else was going wrong.

Immediately, Cyril took his pulse. His heart was racing. From the way the man was breathing, Cyril knew he was in pain.

Cyril took the man's foot in his hand and bent it a little. The muscles in the man's leg started to contract and spasm rapidly. The man flinched away from his touch, but Cyril couldn't tell if it was because he was scared or in pain.

I didn't give him anything that acts on serotonin. The only other thing it could be, really, considering the circumstance, is withdrawal.

Withdrawal made sense given what he'd seen so far. Who knew what the man had been given to make him stay wherever he'd been kept?

"It's okay. I know you're in a lot of pain right now. We can do something to ease all these horrible things you're feeling."

The man looked at him, afraid and reluctant.

"These meds are going to make you feel sleepy, but they'll relax the muscles in your legs." Cyril bent down to his level before the man could put up any sort of protest.

"Listen. I know your type." Technically a lie, but Cyril was going on his best guess of what the man would say in response if he could speak. "You don't need to suffer like this. I don't know what you're withdrawing from. I wish you could tell me, but it's okay that you can't." Again, a lie. "I know you could get through this on your own, but you don't have to. I won't do anything unless you nod your head. You don't have to walk this path alone."

A look of consideration flashed over the man's face, before he nodded very slightly. Cyril considered getting additional confirmation from the man, but decided against it. Just that small nod must've been difficult for him.

Cyril remembered a small bottle of lorazepam he used to have for situations like this. He drew up a very small amount in the smallest syringe he could find.

The look of horror in the man's eyes when he saw the needle hurt Cyril's heart.

"Are you sure?"

This time, the man nodded a bit more frantically and looked away. Cyril nodded a little to himself before he pumped the lorazepam through the man's line.

***

By the third day, the man's condition was getting much better. He was responding well to the therapy with lorazepam and the antibiotics were working quickly to clear the infection. Thankfully, the man hadn't been septic when Cyril found him. Cyril assumed that he'd been severely dehydrated at the time, and the fluids had revived him. Cyril still had no clue what the man was withdrawing from, but he figured that he could wean him off the lorazepam in about a week's time.

The man was complacent when Cyril changed his bandages. Things were looking up for the man. Cyril was relieved beyond words. He'd done the right thing. The man would survive. He didn't let another one die.

The nights were growing colder. It was only normal for the time of year. Cyril started building fires once the man's fear had come down.

On the second day, Cyril had come back from outside to see the man huddled by the fireplace instead of in his bed. Cyril had removed his IV line, but still worried about the injuries being shifted so much.

However, even after he kept putting the man back in bed, he always found him back by the fireplace.

The entire time, other than the little yelp of the first day, the man hadn't made a sound. Instead, he sat there and watched the flames quietly.

Cyril wondered what shapes the fire took on in the man's eyes. Was he replaying memories? Did he see where he came from? What Cyril would've paid to know what was going through his rescue's head.

After three days of silence with another person in the house, Cyril was really struggling with not knowing what to call the man.

He knew absolutely nothing about him, other than he was clearly hooked on something. Cyril thought about the type of person who would do something like what happened to the man to someone. Maybe the silence was something that was trained into the man? Maybe he was taught not to give any details away?

Cyril had a sneaking suspicion that the medication that the man was withdrawing from was, in reality, an antipsychotic. Probably one of the older ones. Thinking over the behavior of the man from before and the withdrawal with the twitching and dizziness and nausea, he thought that whoever kept him probably used it as a sort of chemical restraint.

He absolutely hated the idea. It made him beyond angry. The shock collar, the chemical restraint, the scars from cuffs and whips, all of it. All of it made Cyril hate people more. It reminded him of why he'd left people behind for good.

Fucking sicko.

One thing was clear to Cyril, though. He had a duty to protect the man who he'd found dying in the forest.

If he was going to do that successfully, he needed to figure out a few things. First things first, something to call the man in absence of a name. It felt wrong to not use the man's name directly, but Cyril had a feeling that he wouldn't get a name out of the man for a long time. Thus, he wanted to call him something more human than just ... "his rescue" or "the man he'd found dying who was now living in his house."

Then he needed to figure out whether or not he could talk in a mechanical sense. Cyril had no doubt that mental trauma was playing a role, but he needed to know if it was a brain injury that prevented him from talking – whether from electrocution or blunt force.

Lastly, he wanted to figure out where to return the man to. He didn't want to just drop him off at any police station he found. They'd surely interrogate him and make him horribly uncomfortable, if not completely retraumatize him. Cyril had seen it plenty of times while he was a doctor. Calling the police almost never crossed his mind then, and it hadn't crossed his mind until now.

The system tended to make things worse, not better. If there was anyone who knew that, Cyril would certainly be the one.

No, he needed to figure it out on his own.

As he brought dinner over to the man, Cyril noticed that he'd fallen into a deep sleep. Reluctant to wake him, Cyril sat beside him at the fireplace, eating his fried meat and vegetables.

As he ate, watching the oddly calm visage of the man bathed in the warm light of the flames, he began to wonder if he even had a home to go back to. After all, he ended up with his captor somehow. Would it be cruel to try to bring him somewhere he didn't want to go?

Cyril concluded that he wouldn't worry about it until the man was talking to him. It would be much easier than speculation.

His dirty brown hair flowed around his face, obscuring his eyes a bit. Cyril didn't even realize when he woke up until he moved ever so slightly.

"Shadow."

The man looked at him, confused.

"You're like a little shadow, here, by the fireplace."

The man looked terrified at Cyril's explanation. *Probably afraid he did something wrong, poor thing.*

"It's a good thing, I promise." Not exactly the truth, but not exactly a lie, either. "I'm trying to figure out what to call you."

The terrified expression didn't leave. Cyril frowned. Speculation of what had upset the man rushed through his head, all of which he quickly pushed away. Instead, he handed the man his dinner. The portion was a little bigger than the last – a gradual reintroduction to food.

"Here, eat."

The man took the command well.

Shadow really does suit him.

He watched Cyril carefully, mimicking his actions and eating how he ate. It made Cyril a little sad, how desperately the man was trying to please him.

"Hey, uh." He would've used a name if that wasn't what he was trying to figure out. "Can I, uh, call you Shadow? Until I know your name. You're just, um, very, uh ... shadow-like. Like I said, not a bad thing. Just something I've noticed. I don't want to call you something you don't want to be called, though. So, is Shadow okay?"

After a moment's consideration, the man nodded a little more strongly than before.

CHAPTER 4

One of the most important lessons Sacha ever learned was to never trust the wind. He'd known that lesson long before Master, but Master taught him that sometimes, the wind was a person.

Like the Witch of November, a brisk breeze could so easily become a powerful gale. And, just like the lakes upon which the Witch would reap, Master left no prisoners once a boat's hull was punctured.

One mistake was all it took for that horrible chain of events. That day, it was a simple drop of his fork. Sacha had food on his fork, but Master was making him eat with an injured hand and he couldn't stabilize himself.

Master picked up the fork and took his plate of food away, much to Sacha's dismay.

"Are you so ungrateful as to drop your food?"

Sacha shook his head frantically, whining a little. Master gave him a sharp backhand that brought tears to his eyes.

"I've had a bad enough day without an ungrateful little shit like you wasting good food."

Sacha wanted to beg for mercy, but Master had made clear that he didn't want to hear Sacha do anything, much less *talk*.

"You're pathetic."

Master pulled an all-too-familiar remote from his pocket. He showed it to Sacha. The dial was in the lower range of the remote. "See? I'm normally merciful. I don't even have it very high."

Master cranked the dial all the way to the opposite end of the remote. Before Sacha could do anything, he pressed the button, sending Sacha straight to the ground, screaming and spasming.

His scream was an awful thing. He couldn't even claw at his throat like he wanted to, though the feeling of the prongs heating and burning his skin was distinct. He couldn't breathe. He couldn't make sense of anything. He could only lie there and hope for it to end.

By the time the shocks let up, Sacha was on the verge of fainting. Master didn't seem pleased.

"I've told you once, Sacha." His voice was dangerous. "I won't tell you again after this." Master grabbed his chin, slapping away his tears so they wouldn't touch his hand. "I don't fucking care how painful it is. You are to be silent. Perfectly so."

He threw Sacha back and pressed the button again. Sacha couldn't help but scream again, his throat going raw.

Master repeated the shocks time and time again, until Sacha screamed and cried so much he couldn't even muster a whimper. He wouldn't be able to talk – not for a while. His throat was painful and awfully raw. Sacha could only cough a bit to make it more comfortable. Master would never give him water after a punishment.

"I hope you remember this, Sacha. I never want to hear you again. You're worth less than the food you just dropped."

As Master left with the meal, Sacha could only muster one, lonesome tear when he was finally alone.

***

On the seventh day, Shadow seemed to have mostly recovered from the illness from his wounds. Cyril decided to keep him on antibiotics for a few more days, just to ensure that he had well and truly cleared the infection, but was relieved. He didn't have a fever anymore and the withdrawal was easing with the medication. Cyril was hopeful to get Shadow off of the lorazepam within a week.

Still, Shadow seemed to spend all his time watching the fire. He was perfectly silent at all times, even when he got up to use the restroom. It sort of scared Cyril, how perfectly silent his steps were. He never knew if Shadow was behind him or back in his warm spot by the fireplace.

He was also learning things that scared the man. For one, the element really, really scared him. Cyril had avoided cooking on the stove if Shadow was awake. He couldn't bear to watch Shadow panic every time it crackled to life.

Another thing that scared Shadow was mealtimes themselves. He was always trembling and looked at Cyril with caution, almost as if he'd take the food away. Cyril had started leaving Shadow to eat on his own, too afraid of scaring him and limiting his appetite to sit and eat with him.

Cyril's bedroom seemed to scare him now, too. Cyril had his suspicions as to why, but he didn't ever bring them up. If he would ask what happened, he would never make Shadow divulge something so traumatic

It took a lot of courage for Cyril to decide that he would need to talk to Shadow about mealtimes and cooking. The idea of asking anything and not giving Shadow the proper time to get the courage to express it himself made Cyril uneasy, but he couldn't keep moving mealtimes around. Eventually, produce and meat would spoil.

Deciding how to go about it was difficult, too.

I can't just approach him outright without telling him that I won't hurt him.

Would he even believe me?

Am I overthinking this? He's clearly strong. He's anxious, but he has medicine. He should be able to handle this.

After a long time of thinking, Cyril decided that he would approach Shadow the next day, after his time in the garden.

***

Sacha couldn't remember a time when he'd been given three meals a day and medicine for his mental and physical ailments.

Well, maybe he could, but that time, even if three years wasn't that long in the span of an entire life, seemed like forever ago.

At first, Sacha had worried that he'd misread Cyril and hadn't figured out his needs properly. Sacha quickly came to the conclusion that Cyril wasn't like Master. Master liked his playthings in a constant state of injury. Maybe Cyril enjoyed a fight or preferred his playthings pretty, Sacha thought.

He sure hoped that Cyril wasn't looking for a fight out of him. He wouldn't be able to. He'd be forced back with Master, maybe. Or maybe Master had given him to Cyril for a little while to let him heal.

Sacha thought back to what Cyril had told him. *Whoever kept you, I'm not related to them. I won't do anything to harm you.*

Could that really be true? Could Sacha live a life without being hurt? It seemed impossible. It was impossible.

However, his healing wounds and full belly told him a different story. Cyril hadn't drugged him.

Chlorpromazine. Cyril had wanted to know the name of the medicine that Master used. Maybe he wanted to order some for himself. Since Sacha didn't know if Cyril was his new Master or if he'd go back to Master, he wouldn't say the name. He wouldn't say anything. He couldn't.

Cyril went out the same time, every day. He knew Sacha was good and wouldn't try to run away. *Even if I ended up with him because I ran away.*

Something told Sacha that Cyril would have a much easier time finding him than Master would. The punishment, Sacha imagined, would be worse, too.

So, he'd be good. He wouldn't put up a fight, not unless that was what Cyril wanted from him. Though Sacha got the feeling that, if anything, Cyril preferred him to be codependent.

One day, when Cyril finally came back from outside, he brought a small bowl of fruit. *Cranberries.*

They were Sacha's favorite, but he would never let Cyril know that. He didn't want the cranberries to be used against him. He couldn't have food used against him. Not now. Not ever again.

"Here. I don't know if you like cranberries raw, but they make a decent snack if you can stand their taste."

He handed the bowl to Sacha. It took everything for Sacha to hide his excitement. He hadn't eaten a bowl of cranberries in three years. Having them again was like fruit from the heavens itself.

Once Sacha was about a quarter of the way through the bowl, Cyril cleared his throat. Sacha snapped to attention, putting the bowl down. He knew it was rude to eat while someone else was talking.

"Shadow, I – um." Cyril took a deep breath. To his surprise, Sacha didn't really feel scared. He knew it was the medicine that Cyril was giving him. "I had a question for you. It's just a yes-no question and whatever you indicate won't upset me. I mean no harm, okay? I'm only trying to understand something."

Sacha waited patiently for Cyril to continue.

"Okay." Cyril looked like he was having trouble putting his words together. Sacha found it odd – he was just a slave. He wasn't worthy of such nerves. "Whenever I turn on the burner to cook food, you seem to have a panic attack or something close to it."

Sacha froze.

No.

No.

No.

No.

Please don't hurt me. I can't help it.

Please.

"I promise you I'm not angry." Sacha found no comfort in those words. "I just want to know something. When I was taking care of your wounds and hooking you up to the IV, when you were passed out, you had a shock collar on. Are you scared that I'm going to electrocute you?"

Sacha's blood ran cold. He suddenly didn't know what to think. In fact, his mind had gone totally blank.

Memories rushed back to him. He touched a hand to the bandaged burns on his throat.

Of course he figured it out.

Wait.

He took my collar off. Does he know that I belong to Master, then? He has to know that Master doesn't ever want my collar to come off.

The answer was suddenly obvious.

Sacha was never going back to Master.

Cyril was his new Master. There was no other way Cyril would keep him.

Tears formed in Sacha's eyes. His chest grew tight. The medicine that Cyril had given him made it easier to cry. It made Sacha feel absolutely pathetic. He didn't want to make a sound. He didn't want to upset Cyril by crying.

Cyril, for his part, looked terribly uncomfortable. Sacha was going to get a punishment. He knew it. He'd made his new master uncomfortable. Should he apologize? He didn't know what his new master wanted out of him.

"Shadow, listen to me."

Sacha snapped back to attention, fighting back the tears that wanted to spill so badly.

"I'm sorry for being so straightforward."

Don't apologize to me.

"It's okay to cry."

No, it isn't. Slaves don't cry.

"Just nod yes or no for me. Just let me know, then I'll be done. Okay?"

It was impossibly merciful, yet so, so impossible. Sacha knew he was doing nothing to impress his new master, but he *had* to obey orders. He needed to show, at the very least, that he could listen when given the opportunity.

He nodded a bit. He was scared of being electrocuted each time he heard the element come to life.

Cyril nodded a bit, before he wrapped his arms around Sacha.

Sacha flinched away at first, before he realized what Cyril was doing.

A hug?

He was undeserving.

“Shhh, it’s okay, Shadow.”

Those words were impossible to believe.

“Please, let out what you need to. It’s okay to cry. You’ve been through so much. I’m so sorry that all this has happened to you. There’s nothing I can do to make it better, but please, just cry. Don’t force yourself to hold your tears back.”

That, Sacha could listen to. He sobbed his perfectly silent sobs, his breath catching in his throat. He didn’t know how long he cried for, but Sacha did know one thing. It felt damn good to let the floodgates open, if only for a brief moment in time.

Chapter 5

Throughout the next few days, Cyril began to notice small things wrong with his setup. He'd never expected to have another person in his little cabin, much less someone he'd need to treat.

First, he was running out of medicines. Now that he was treating someone with injuries and trauma, he needed much more than just his bottles of paracetamol, ibuprofen, and diphenhydramine.

He'd managed to convince himself that he could tough it out with just his leftovers, but as time crawled on, he realized he couldn't.

Once he realized that he would eventually need to go into town to get medicine, small problems started to appear everywhere. His blankets were too old. His pillows were too flat. His watering can had a hole in it.

Shadow was sleeping on the couch in front of the fireplace, too. He'd refused pillows in his own way. Blankets, too, eventually. Cyril would walk in on him sleeping on the couch with those borrowed, far too big clothes, nothing else. It wasn't healthy. He needed a bed, even if getting him to use it would be a challenge in itself.

Dread filled Cyril's stomach as he realized he needed to go into town.

"Fuck!"

He really didn't like going into town. They all knew him there because of his biyearly visits. To make an extra trip would cause so much commotion.

Cyril wanted to scream.

Instead, he decided to very angrily pull weeds from the flower bed. He didn't want to scare Shadow by screaming.

Shadow looked at him with that all-too-familiar fear in his eyes when Cyril finally went back inside.

"I need to shower."

It was true. He was covered in mud. However, he needed to calm down more than he needed to shower. Shadow just watched him quietly as he prepared his money and bags for the town. Just as he left, he remembered to grab a small piece of paper that sat buried in a drawer. Cyril's mood soured as he looked at it.

***

His first stop in the town was the pharmacy. The pharmacist was someone he knew somewhat well – an older lady with a knack for sniffing out a lies, gossip and not much else. It was perhaps a good decision to have her as the pharmacist. After all, people were always looking for their next fix. In such a miserable world, Cyril didn't blame them.

"Well, you're a sight for sore eyes," she said immediately upon seeing him.

Cyril tried his best to at least seem amicable. "Been busy."

"Mhm, I bet." She looked at him with mild amusement, which just pissed Cyril off. "What can I do for you?"

Cyril put down the piece of paper he'd grabbed from his drawer. "I need medicine."

"A doctor?" She scoffed. "What are you doing living in the middle of the forest? You could have so much more."

Cyril tried to keep the anger off his face. "Mind your own damn business."

"Really, now?" She took his advice despite the disapproval and didn't press further. "What can I get you, Dr. Galanos?"

Cyril took a deep breath, his brow twitching a bit. "I need lorazepam, thirty 0.5 milligram pills, cefdinir, thirty 300 milligram pills, and 300-30 milligram paracetamol-codeine, thirty pills."

"You'll need to fill out a lot of paperwork for that order. I hope to God you're not using lorazepam with the codeine."

Cyril had many unkind things to say, none of which would actually get him the medicine he needed. "I know what I'm – " He paused. "Doing. Throw some bisacodyl and loperamide in there while you're at it. As many as you can give me."

She nodded and handed him the paperwork. Admittedly, he'd moved to the area because of their loose dispensary laws. It allowed him to get what he needed without much interaction. However, even paperwork like what he was filling out: the condition, time period, so on and so forth, was draining.

Once he was done with the papers, she went in the back and rounded up the medicine for him. She knew there wasn't a point making him wait until the next day – he'd never come and she'd lose the sale. He quietly handed her the money and headed out to the next store.

***

The carpenter raised an eyebrow at Cyril.

"You need what now?"

"Lumber." Cyril explained exactly how much he needed. "My cabin needs repairs."

It was a lie. Cyril didn't want to have to spend money on transport and setup of a commercial mattress frame, so he'd decided to build one for Shadow himself. However, he would never tell the villagers that. They'd gossip for days about what lady friend he'd brought over and how the hermit was finally letting people into his house again. For all he knew, they'd start trying to come over themselves!

"We can have someone come out there to fix it for you."

"I'd rather not," Cyril said pointedly.

"Alright, then. How do you plan to get it back?"

"I'm renting a car from the mechanic."

The carpenter nodded. "Sounds good to me. Do you need anything else besides this lumber? Nails? Tools? Anything of the sort?"

"No. Just the lumber." It came out more sharply than Cyril had intended.

"Alright, you bring the car around. I'll have my guys load it all in for you once they're done prepping it for you."

Cyril was about to say something, but in the end, he was pleasantly surprised by how polite and non-intrusive the carpenter was. "Thank you."

As he was leaving, he turned around. "Do you know where I could get a mattress here?"

"A mattress?"

"Yes, your mattress breaks every once and a while."

The carpenter went a little quiet. "Drive about a mile out of here and you'll see this mattress store. It's very out of the way, but you'll find it. They should have something you can install yourself, since I know you prefer that."

Cyril nodded a bit. "Thank you, again. I hope you have a good day."

"You as well."

CHAPTER 6

"*Please*, Master, I'm very hungry."

Sacha was down on his knees, bowing down to the monster who called him a pet. His hunger was an empty pit in his stomach that only grew bigger by the hour. When was the last time that Master had fed him?

A sharp backhand interrupted his thoughts.

"Who told you that you could speak?"

Master grabbed his chin and tilted his head up. The controlled, furious glare in Master's eyes was unmistakable.

He growled a little when Sacha flinched back from his touch. "I fucking told you, Sacha, you don't talk. I never want to hear you. I don't care if you're hungry. I don't care if you're in pain. I don't care what the reason is. I never want you to speak."

There were tears in Sacha's eyes as Master left the room. The lights stayed on, which meant that he was certainly coming back.

When Master came back with that eye-of-the-hurricane calm, cane in hand, Sacha whimpered.

Master took the cane and hit Sacha across the face where he'd been struck earlier. It was everything he could do to not cry out again. He could feel the bruises forming on every inch of injured skin.

"Hands out."

Sacha couldn't do it. It was so impossible, knowing that he would be caned on his hands and wrists.

Master struck him again with the cane on his face.

"I said put your hands out, pet."

When Sacha didn't put his hands out, Master grabbed and pulled with the strength to rip his arms out.

Immediately, he released the cane on the gentle skin of his wrists. Sacha did his best to keep his whimpers in as blow after blow came down until the cane began to break the skin of his wrists. Eventually, his blood splattered on the cane and Master's hands.

After what felt like thirty blows, Master stopped and left again. The lights were still on, though Master left for a long time.

Sacha stayed in position, too scared to upset Master if he did anything without permission.

Master came back. The smell of warm food filled the room. Chicken with potatoes, maybe.

Master tilted Sacha's chin up, looking at his wounds. "I didn't mean to go that far." He put a hand to Sacha's face and wiped the tears off Sacha's face. "Let me fix that for you."

He took soft bandages out of his pocket and gently, tenderly, began to wrap Sacha's wrists. He was careful not to apply too much pressure, so as not to hurt Sacha.

Sacha hated how he leaned into the gentle touch. He hated that he found comfort in it.

"All of this could've been avoided, Sacha. If only you'd just been quiet, I wouldn't have had to do this." Master pet Sacha's hair. "You took your punishment very well. You were quiet, like you were supposed to be."

He took the plate of food from the floor beside him. It was a simple meal of half a chicken breast, half a potato, and a few string beans.

Quietly, Master fed him small bites. It wasn't seasoned well, but Sacha found himself not caring. He was simply too hungry. Anything would've been an elixir of the gods.

***

Sacha had noticed a few things about his new Master. For once, Cyril didn't seem to ever go interact with other people. He was unlike Master, who had people over every day, it seemed. Cyril was perfectly content with going out to garden or sometimes coming back to the cabin with new meat and furs.

When he left, he didn't give Sacha any talk about having to stay. Did he know that Sacha would obey? Well, Sacha had had plenty of chances to escape at that point. Every day, Cyril left for hours at a time. If he wanted to escape, he could've easily then.

Why don't I want to escape?

It was a question that had been bothering Sacha. He felt no will to leave the cabin. Maybe some part of him believed that Cyril owning him was protecting him from returning to Master. Master was worlds worse than Cyril, even if Sacha didn't know what he wanted. Cyril hadn't hit him yet. Cyril hadn't asked for anything, really, in fact. Maybe it was because he enjoyed the complete reliance Sacha had on him.

When he heard a commotion outside, Sacha dared to peek out the front door's window.

Cyril was in a car, unloading lumber, a box, and a bag from the trunk.

He said he was getting things for me.

Guilt panged in his chest. Had he really looked so awful that Cyril had taken it upon himself to get such extravagances for him?

I'm awful.

Sacha knew he'd have to pay for his awfulness in blood. He waited in his spot by the fireplace. When Cyril entered, he was annoyed. Sacha could tell immediately.

Tears sprung to his eyes.

The gentle man was going to hurt him. Sacha got into position, holding out his scarred wrists.

Yet Cyril walked right past him into one of the storage closets.

Maybe the punishment is for later.

Right, I'm so stupid. It isn't my job to decide when I'll be punished.

Slowly, piece by piece, Cyril brought the lumber into the cabin. The sun was beginning to set in the distance. Sacha didn't realize the tension he was carrying in his body until he moved to the couch quietly, like Cyril had told him to when he was tired. Cyril came over and gently lifted the blanket onto him.

"Rest well, Shadow."

As Sacha fell asleep, he couldn't fathom the kind gesture when all he deserved was punishment.

***

Sacha was awoken in the middle of the night by the sound of nailing. Immediately, he froze.

No.

No.

No. I don't want nails. He can't be that cruel.

Sacha whipped his head around, looking in every direction to see where the nailing was coming from. His limbs didn't hurt, so he wasn't the thing being nailed.

Eventually, he noticed Cyril, bent over a pile of wood that looked vaguely like *a bed frame?*

"Sorry, Shadow. I couldn't sleep."

Why are you apologizing? If this is the punishment you're giving me ...

Well, he couldn't fight, could he?

Cyril squinted at him. "You look afraid. Are you okay?"

It was an impossible question. Of course he was afraid. Did Cyril want him to look happy for his punishments? Even if that's what Cyril wanted, Sacha wasn't sure he could muster the courage to do as he was told, if it meant looking happy for that.

"Of course not." Cyril chuckled mirthlessly. "I must have scared you. It's okay. I'm just building your bed over here. I know you don't want to be anywhere near mine, but it isn't healthy for you to keep sleeping on the couch. Bad for your neck."

Oh, how Sacha wanted to protest that he wasn't worthy of the couch, much less his own bed. He wouldn't show such flagrant disobedience, though.

"Just ... go back to sleep if you can, Sacha."

Cyril came over to where Sacha laid. As he brought the blanket that had been tossed to the side over Sacha's body, Sacha flinched and whimpered a bit.

Sacha froze. He'd made a noise. Panic rose in his chest. He didn't want to be punished, not while the nails were out. God, he was going to have a nail through his hand, wasn't he?

Cyril pulled away for a moment. Sacha watched between rushed breaths and teary eyes as he went to the kitchen and returned with a candy bar. He took it out of its wrapper and took out a piece of chocolate. Cyril handed it off to Sacha.

"Here, put this in your mouth."

Sacha didn't want to listen and accept another kindness, knowing that he would pay for it later, but his will to obey was greater than any fear of punishment.

"Good, focus on the taste of it. The sweetness. The bitterness."

He didn't know why his new Master was so intent on helping him, but Sacha still obeyed. He rolled the chocolate around in his mouth and, with a pang of guilt, found himself enjoying it.

Cyril gently carded a hand through Sacha's hair once he was calmer. Sacha did his best not to flinch away.

"You're doing well, Shadow."

Sacha had a very difficult time believing that.

***

When Sacha woke up, he wasn't quite sure when he'd fallen asleep. He took a panicked look around and realized that he was, in fact, uninjured and still in his clothes.

Cyril didn't do anything.

It's okay. He wasn't mad at me.

Sacha knew he'd earned a punishment. He knew that Cyril would punish him eventually. But for now, he was okay. He was safe while Cyril wasn't around.

He got off of his spot on the couch and moved back to his seat by the fireplace. Cyril had put him in charge of tending to it. He was happy to serve his new Master, so he always listened and threw in more wood.

How long he sat there and watched it, he didn't know, but eventually, his safety was gone. His new Master had awoken from his slumber and had come to see him.

"Good morning, Shadow," he said with a yawn in his voice.

Something felt disrespectful about being silent and motionless, but Sacha did as he was taught.

Cyril approached him quietly. "When ... did you last wash?"

Sacha froze. He didn't think that Cyril would care. Master didn't. Master had washed him when it pleased him and no other time.

He found an old impulse to apologize, but kept silent.

"Right, you don't talk."

Cyril said it ... almost as if it was a bad thing.

"Come on, let's get you washed up. I promise I'm not angry, just a little confused."

Sacha nodded and followed Cyril to the bathroom. A flush came to his cheeks as he stripped down to get in the bath.

"Um, not yet. I was going to draw a bath for you, unless you'd prefer a shower."

Sacha had no preferences. He was a slave. Whatever his new Master wanted him to have was what he would have.

Cyril handed Sacha a fluffy towel. "We can do a shower, if that's what you prefer."

Shorter. Less chances for Sacha to mess up something. Less chances for him to earn an even worse punishment.

Cyril motioned for Sacha to come to the tap. "What water do you use?"

It was an easy test. Sacha only ever used cold water. He turned the water up a bit to the coldest setting and left it running.

Cyril nodded a bit, knowingly. "So, you only use cold water?"

Yes. Sacha was a good slave.

Cyril, despite everything, sighed a bit. "Okay, Shadow. Please, shower in warm water. It's okay."

Sacha didn't believe him. It couldn't be right. It was just a test, another one, to see if he knew his place.

"Alright, come into the shower," Cyril said while he turned the water up.

Sacha flinched as he stepped into the shower. The water had to be scalding. This had to be his punishment.

It's warm.

It wasn't hot. It wasn't cold. Just pleasantly warm.

Sacha was flabbergasted, but didn't doubt what his new Master was doing.

Gently, careful not to get a drop of water in his face, Cyril rinsed down his hair. Then, with the same care, he massaged Sacha's scalp with shampoo. Sacha couldn't help but feel himself relax a bit into the tender touch.

"You have dandruff. Poor thing."

It was true that his scalp had been itchy.

"Probably all that stress. I'm sorry."

Why is he apologizing?

Not a drop of soap got into his eyes as Cyril rinsed out his hair.

Soon after, Cyril lathered the washcloth and handed it to Sacha. Sacha obediently, carefully washed himself down, avoiding his wounds like Cyril had instructed.

Cyril rinsed him off in that pleasantly warm water. Sacha was undeserving. He would pay for it later, but he tried not to think about it. He didn't dare hope anymore. That had long been crushed out of him. However, if this new Master of his wanted to pamper him once in a while, even if he had to pay for it later, Sacha could learn to bear it. Maybe he'd even come to enjoy tender moments between the painful ones.

Chapter 7

Something about having a bed to go to was almost unbelievable. Sacha had spent so long, naked on the cold, cement floor of a dark, dank basement that to have someone tuck him in and wish him sweet dreams felt surreal.

The covers to his new bed were freshly washed and warm. The smell and feel of them, the soft, plush fabric of the duvet brought tears to his eyes. He felt unworthy, yet so comfortable. He felt guilty, but couldn't bring himself to move, not yet.

Once Cyril had gone to bed, Sacha allowed his eyes to wander back to the fireplace. He didn't expect to dislike being away from it so much.

He told me to stay in this bed. I can't disobey.

Another thought occurred to Sacha.

What if this is a test? What if he's trying to see if I know my place? Test my limits?

Every bone in his body ached, as though the fatigue of the years past was tying him down to that bed. Even though his bones ached, his muscles were relaxed. Was this what it was like to rest?

Sacha knew that fear was the normal state of affairs for a slave, but he enjoyed allowing himself to relax a bit. However, enjoyment was an emotion for someone worth much more than he was. He quickly summoned that fear by pinching the scars on his wrists.

It hit him like a tidal wave. His chest tightened. Suddenly, he was back with Master. Master was towering in front of him, willow cane in hand. Tears were running down his face. He was going to be punished. He was going to be punished. He was going to *hurt* and *pay* for the kindness he'd been shown.

Sacha got up from his bed, leaving all the blankets behind. The scars on his wrists burned horribly like fire scorching his skin, through his nerves, and into his mind.

This has to be a test. He wants to know if I know my place.

It broke Sacha's heart to not be able to sleep in that beautiful bed. However, he was determined to prove to his new Master that he was well trained, that he didn't need to be trained again or sent back to Master.

He moved to his spot by the fireplace, dutifully tending to the flames. Comfort washed over Sacha as he sat by the hearth, watching those flames dance. He had control over the fire. The fire would not hurt him, so long as he didn't tempt it. It was entirely different from human beings – unpredictable, awful creatures that could hurt him at any moment.

Sacha fell asleep that night, deep into the evening hours, listening to the crackling of the fresh wood in the hearth.

***

Cyril woke with a start and immediately turned his head to his alarm clock. *2:13.*

Fuck.

His heart was beating out of his chest. When he looked at his hand, it was trembling.

Cyril forced himself to take a few deep breaths. It was just a nightmare. It couldn't hurt him. No matter how real it felt, it couldn't do anything to him. Some part of him couldn't believe that the nightmare was, in fact, just a nightmare, but he told himself that it was just his mind playing tricks on him.

He eventually decided to go to the kitchen and make himself a warm glass of hot cocoa. Cyril hadn't made a glass for himself after a nightmare in what felt like a long time.

However, when he left his room, he remembered exactly *why* that was. Shadow was asleep beside the fireplace, not a single blanket or pillow in sight.

I thought that I made him a bed?

Cyril looked at the wall where he'd positioned Shadow's bed. It was certainly still there.

Why is he sleeping on the floor?

What Cyril would have paid to know what was going through Shadow's head.

If only he could talk. It would make things so much easier.

Cyril was no mind reader. Even if he was halfway decent at reading people and figuring out their intentions, he couldn't look into the deepest parts of a person like that.

Even if he could, would he?

Wouldn't that be horribly violating Shadow's privacy?

Cyril had never thought about mind reading like that. However, the thought of somebody reading into his thoughts and memories was deeply disturbing.

Cyril forced himself to focus on the task at hand.

I'll talk to him in the morning.

There wasn't any sense in waking Shadow up to discuss something that would probably end up deeply upsetting to the both of them.

Cyril glanced once more to the kitchen. He didn't feel like making hot cocoa anymore, so he headed back to his bedroom. Sleep found him almost as soon as his head hit the pillow.

***

Shadow awoke before him, like he usually did. Cyril decided to make them both breakfast before he brought up how he'd found Shadow sleeping.

Breakfast was a simple one – applesauce, oatmeal, milk, and maple syrup. Shadow seemed to enjoy it well enough.

"Shadow."

Cyril's heart broke when Shadow gave him a fearful look. Granted, he should have been used to seeing fear in those light hazel eyes. It seemed to be one of the only two emotions that Shadow knew well.

Cyril steadied himself before he found the courage to bring the subject up. "I found you sleeping on the floor last night." He had to think over his words so that they wouldn't sound like an admonishment. "I'm not upset with you, I promise. Just ... I made you a bed because I wanted you to sleep somewhere nice. I didn't want you to sleep on the floor."

Shadow looked like a kicked puppy. Something in that fear told Cyril that Shadow didn't really know what he did wrong.

It was hard to convince him to sleep on the couch. Plus, when he'd first brought Shadow home, he'd refused to rest in bed.

"Shadow, you're allowed to sleep in that bed. It's yours. It's not mine."

Cyril didn't know how to convince Shadow that no ill would befall him from sleeping in the bed. In fact, he was a little exasperated.

"I worked hard to make it. Please, use it. I ... I don't like going into town. Just please use it, okay?"

Shadow made no indication either way, except for the tears that were brimming in his eyes. Cyril felt awful.

Dammit. I made him cry.

What was he supposed to do? He was the reason that Shadow was crying. Shadow probably didn't want his comfort.

Thus, Cyril decided it was probably for the best if he just left. It felt so horrible and cruel to leave Shadow alone, but he was beginning to realize that Shadow was something of a solitary creature. He probably would prefer to be alone for a little while to calm down before Cyril tried talking to him again.

He took a deep breath and rounded up his gardening materials. He'd think better once he was out in his garden, anyway.

***

I failed.

The thought permeated everything as Sacha found his place by the fireplace. He'd failed the test that Cyril had set up for him.

Sobs formed in his chest. How was he supposed to pass all these little tests when everything was so different from the way it had been with Master?

Sacha curled up in a ball and cried into his knees for a long time.

So long, in fact, that Cyril returned home in the meantime.

Sacha looked up at him with red-rimmed eyes, wanting to throw himself on his knees and *beg* for the punishment he deserved.

"Hey, Shadow. I'm sorry. I was too harsh with you earlier."

Something inside Sacha curled up. *No. Don't apologize to me.*

Am I really that pathetic?

God, I'm awful.

I'm horrible.

I'm going to be sent back.

I don't deserve his kindness.

"Listen, I've realized something."

Sacha looked up at him intently, tears rolling down his face. Cyril paused for a moment and grabbed a blanket off the bed. Gently, he wrapped Sacha in it and pulled him into a hug.

"You feel better over here."

It was true. The fireplace was precious to Sacha. Not only was it his only job, it was also his only protection.

"I want you to be happy here."

It couldn't be possible.

"So, I'm going to move your bed by the fireplace, okay? That way, you know it's for you and you can feel safe over here."

Sacha didn't know what to say.

Why is he being so kind to me?

Nothing made sense anymore. At least with Master, before he was Cyril's, he knew what he needed to do. Be silent and please Master well. With Cyril, he was expected to be *happy*. How in the world could he ever be happy again? What was happiness if life was so awful?

Cyril let him go from his hug and held true to his word. Without Sacha's help, he moved the couch to where the bed was and moved the bed to where the couch was.

Tears – relieved, confused ones this time – rolled down his face as Cyril took a deep breath, before pulling him back into a hug. He didn't force Sacha away from his safe spot on the floor as he hugged him, sitting there by the fire with him.

"You didn't do anything wrong, okay? I'm still figuring this all out, Shadow. I'm sorry that I can't always get it right. We'll get through this. You're here to heal. I promise that I will never hurt you, okay? I promise I would never do anything like that."

Sacha found himself wanting to thank Cyril. The thought was odd. He genuinely wanted to thank Cyril for giving him so much consideration. He didn't want to thank Cyril for not hurting him. No, he wanted to thank him for the bed, the food, and the gentle care.

It felt almost like life before, as though the bed were a present and the food was a home-cooked meal.

Sacha quickly put the thought out of his head.

He refused.

He couldn't hope for anything.

However, as he warmed in Cyril's big arms, he began to wonder what exactly healing might feel like. Could the urge to thank Cyril for his kindness be that?

Sacha didn't know.

Chapter 8

Sacha's arms were brought above his head, pulling, pulling his weight below him until his arms were going to fall out of their sockets. His feet were just barely dangling above the ground. It was enough to make him want to scream in pain.

However, screaming was exactly what had landed him in that position.

A loud *snap* came from one of his shoulders. Pain exploded, like a small bomb had forced it out of place, spreading painful shrapnel in its place. Sacha let out a small whimper.

"What did I say, Sacha?"

Master was behind him.

Sacha shrank, pulling on his dislocated shoulder. He got the instinct to run at first, but it was quickly replaced with a paralyzing sort of fear. Sacha watched Master like a deer in the headlights as Master circled him like a vulture.

Master chuckled and tilted Sacha's chin, admiring the bruises on his jaw and the hickeys on his neck.

"You're going to look so beautiful when I'm done with you."

In his hand was a barbed whip. Sacha didn't recognize it at first. Master typically used the cane, not a whip.

"Now, if you're quiet, you might get some food tonight. Alright? Doesn't that sound good?" Master had a wicked smile on his face as he moved around to Sacha's back.

Sacha wanted to plead. He wanted to cry. He wanted to scream. *Something.* He wanted to do something. Yet all he could do was look on in fear. What choice did he have?

Sacha felt the pain of his flesh being torn open before he heard the crack of the whip. He couldn't help himself – he screamed.

"What the fuck did I say about making noise, you piece of shit?"

Master circled around and grabbed Sacha's jaw with bruising force. Sacha shrank back from Master's touch, which only earned him another slap to the face before the iron grip returned, stronger than before.

"I should gag you, but you have to learn to be silent."

Master let go of Sacha and grabbed the remote out of his pocket. The electric shocks started. Sacha was helpless against them, thrashing, wrenching his dislocated shoulder further out of place. Tears quickly formed in his eyes.

Master slapped him again once the shocks were done. "I hope you remember your place."

Sacha nodded frantically, but all it did was earn him another slap.

"You're a slave. You don't have opinions. You don't respond. You're to be quiet and obedient. I don't give a shit about what you think. If I cared, I wouldn't have bought you, now, would I?"

Sacha forced himself to hold back sobs. He hated himself. He hated his situation. He hated that he couldn't follow such simple orders.

I'm so stupid.

The whip was quick to crack on his back again. As it tore up his flesh, he remained perfectly silent, pliant, just as he was told. This was what he deserved, after all, for what he'd done.

What had he done, again?

***

In truth, Cyril didn't buy *just* the materials for the bed when he was in town. He kept a small box in his closet of other things he'd bought for Shadow but wasn't sure about. He wanted to respect Shadow. He didn't want Shadow to feel infantilized by his care.

The line between respectful care and infantilizing seemed thin, even if Cyril knew he was doing the right thing. Maybe he was just anxious. Maybe the situation reminded him just enough of before to trigger his post-traumatic stress. Cyril didn't know what had him so anxious, when care used to come so naturally, but he figured that it was an important line to be aware of.

One of the items in the box was a large bottle of scar cream. The pharmacist had certainly given him an odd look when he'd asked for an extra large bottle of it. Cyril would've normally cared an awful lot about the look, but he brushed it off. Shadow was more important than their gossip, wasn't he?

Cyril didn't know how to approach the topic with Shadow. The man didn't really communicate with him. However, he saw the self-conscious way that Shadow always tried to cover his scars. Scar cream didn't seem like such a bad idea. It might not get rid of the scars entirely, but it could help to reduce the angry look of them.

Part of Cyril felt that he was making the decision for Shadow. Shadow wouldn't say no to anything. How could he know what Shadow wanted?

Cyril decided that if Shadow seemed happy about the scar cream, he would help the man apply it to the worst of his scars.

However, building the courage to ask was a different task. Cyril spent many hours in his garden thinking about how to ask Shadow without putting pressure on him if he didn't want it. Eventually, Cyril decided to rip the band-aid off and deal with whatever happened. No matter how much he thought about it, he couldn't predict how Shadow would react.

"Shadow?"

Shadow snapped to attention from his place beside the fireplace. Cyril hated how Shadow always looked like he'd been hit when he paid attention to what Cyril had to say.

"I – um." Cyril wiped some of the sweat off of his forehead. "I bought scar cream for you in town. I don't want to make that decision for you, but you cover your scars a lot, and I thought that maybe reducing the look of them would help you." Cyril swallowed a bit. "I know this cream. It's really good stuff. It'll definitely make them less noticeable, if that's something you want."

Shadow visually perked up before he went back to the crumpled, sad mess in blankets on the floor. Cyril was beginning to realize that Shadow wasn't just conditioned not to talk, but also to not show any emotions. The thought made him sick.

However, that perk was one of the biggest he'd seen from Shadow. He took that as Shadow genuinely wanting his scars to be reduced. Regardless, the scar cream wouldn't hurt him.

"I'll go get it, okay? We can put it on after I shower."

Again, Shadow was mostly motionless. However, as he turned to his bedroom to go shower, Cyril swore he might've seen a semblance of a smile on Shadow's face.

***

The cream was cool against Sacha's skin. It wasn't slimy, just pleasantly cool, like a balm. Sacha felt himself relaxing a bit with his shirt off as Cyril applied the cream. Master had never done such a thing for him.

This ... probably won't be as bad.

I can bear this. I can bear whatever he does if I can be taken care of after.

Sacha felt some guilt at feeling that his Master had been bad to him. After all, he was a slave, there for another's pleasure. How he was treated was of little consequence. He'd been an awful slave for Master.

However, with Cyril, he might've gotten something right. That gave Sacha hope, hope that he wouldn't screw it all up like he had with Master. He knew he still deserved to pay in blood for the kindness Cyril showed him, but this kindness was so much more *kind* than the kindness Master had given him.

Everything changed when Cyril's hand brushed over a particular scar on his hip bone.

Suddenly, Sacha was right back there with Master, back when he was a disobedient, bad slave.

Master was rubbing a bit of balm over his fresh brand. Sacha let out small curses each time Master hit a particularly deep part of the burn.

Master had been lenient then – not that Sacha didn't pay for it later in blood. However, that night, right after his brand, he'd been allowed to speak.

"Shhh, shhh. I know. I know it hurts. I'm sorry that I had to do this. It's for your own good, Sacha, baby."

"Fuck you, Emery!"

"Be careful, Sacha. Just because I'm allowing you to talk right now doesn't mean that you can squander my kindness."

The memory brought tears to Sacha's eyes. How could he have been so foolish back then? He knew he'd pay for it all later. Why hadn't he just stayed silent? It was so much easier than talking, anyway.

Sacha hated his past self. He hadn't understood his purpose, his place in the world. Regret filled him each time he looked back at the Sacha that shouted and cried and sang and *talked*.

What would Cyril do about the brand? Surely, he couldn't stand another man's mark on his slave. Sacha felt a panic attack forming in his chest. God, Cyril was going to cut it right out of him, wasn't he? He was going to pay for allowing himself to be marked. He was going to pay for being allowed to relax. He was going to pay for the kindness, the bed, and the hot chocolate.

A big, heavy weight fell on his shoulders and covered and warmed his exposed back. Sacha felt Cyril's arms around him, pulling him into a warm hug.

Sacha soon realized that the blanket covering him was heavy and navy blue. Cyril was hugging him and rocking him a bit.

"It's okay, Shadow."

Sacha looked up at him. He'd looked pathetic again, hadn't he? He had stopped his new Master from carrying out another punishment.

Tears filled his eyes. He couldn't hold back his sobs, but at least he could make them silent.

"Shhh, Shadow, you're safe here."

Sacha refused to believe it. He would never be safe. Safety wasn't for slaves like him.

"It's okay to cry. You were whimpering a lot."

Sacha looked up at him, fear overwhelming him. Another panic attack formed in his chest. He'd made noise. He'd made noise. He wasn't quiet. He was going to be punished.

"It's okay, Shadow. I don't mind you ... whimpering. I do mind. I don't like seeing you in pain. But I would never hurt you for that."

Sacha knew they were all lies to get him to trust. Trust, only so his trust could be broken later. That was how people like Cyril liked their slaves, right? Trusting, then untrusting, then trusting again.

"Listen ... none of this is a trick. You're here to *heal*. I'll say it as many times as I need to. It's okay to cry. It's okay to make noise. Okay?"

Sacha was overwhelmed with the urge to obey.

Right. He wants me to be happy sometimes.

Will it hurt more when he betrays me?

Sacha melted in Cyril's arms, under the weight of the blanket that was taking away his worries and calming his panic.

I should enjoy this while it lasts.

Sacha let out a few more broken sobs, allowing Cyril to hug him tighter. Yes, he would enjoy the comfort while it lasted. It was better than pain, after all.

Chapter 9

Dark rooms had long since become a pattern in Sacha's life. First, the dark room where he'd been kept in a cage. Then, the dark rooms he was transported in. Now, the dark room where he laid naked and bound at the wrists.

Sacha hated the dark. He hated the cold. He hated the room. He hated the pain that radiated from every bone in his body. More than anything, he hated himself. How had it all come to this? How had he become a slave to a horrible, cruel man?

His hands might've gone to his collar if they weren't tied behind his back. *His* collar. Tears formed in Sacha's eyes. He really was just a pet, now, wasn't he? Someone else's entirely.

No, Sacha was lower than a pet. He was a slave. He would be branded, tattooed, and forced to bend to the cruel man's will. What was his name again? Emery Abberton?

Bruises around his neck ached around the tightness of the collar. In fact, it had been hard to breathe since Emery had put it on.

Beautiful. You're absolutely beautiful in your collar.

Emery had smiled and stroked his cheek when Sacha cried. He hated the way that after all the beating from the guards at the auction house, he leaned into Emery's touch. He hated the way that Emery had complimented him for his pliant nature, for how good of a pet he would be.

Nobody would think that of him for long. Not if Sacha had anything to do with it. Surely, they couldn't be far from civilization. He could run, if he could only fight off Emery.

In the end, he didn't have much time to think. In fact, he'd hardly slept a wink since his confinement in the dark rooms and the injections of sleeping medicine they'd given him for transport at the auction house.

The door of his cold, dark little room opened and light flooded in. Sacha's eyes hurt as the blinding halogen lights came on in the room. He whimpered a bit, though his eyes were quick to adjust. They would surely not stay that way forever.

"Look at you!" Emery came over and stroked his hair, looking at Sacha's collar with glee. "Only some bruises and you'll be perfect, Sacha."

The idea filled Sacha with primordial fear. What did Emery intend to do with him, exactly? Sacha had some ideas, none of which meant well for him.

Nobody was coming to save him from his fate. That left the responsibility squarely on his shoulders.

Emery stuck two fingers under Sacha's collar, pressing intentionally on the bruises that laid underneath.

"I put that on too tight, poor thing," Emery cooed. "Let me fix that for you. I can't have my latest prize dying."

Emery did exactly that – pulled the collar off, then put it back on a little less tight. Sacha might've been thankful had it not been a *collar*.

Foolishly, Emery went around and undid the restraints that held Sacha's hands back. The moment they were freed, Sacha threw a punch at Emery's face.

He didn't even have time to scream before an unknown, horrible pain lit up every muscle in his body. He collapsed, convulsing and crying as shocks filled every inch of his body. It was white-hot, like burning iron being forced through every muscle in him.

No. No. No. It's a shock collar. It's a shock collar.

Sacha felt himself losing control over everything. He couldn't hold himself together, not in the face of such blinding, mind-numbing pain.

Sobs hiccuped through his body. He couldn't take the pain. He couldn't take being alive. He wanted to die. He'd do anything to die.

***

A pair of hands grabbed Sacha's wrists.

Sacha thrashed against the restraint. He couldn't be kept as a slave forever. He couldn't die belonging to someone else. He couldn't exist just to be used and hurt.

However, Sacha didn't remember Master ever using restraints that didn't hurt. Even as weight held his knees down and pinned his wrists, Sacha wasn't in any pain. In fact, he was in a bed. He wasn't ever in a bed with Master unless ...

"Shadow!"

The familiar voice of his new Master came from above. Sacha's vision cleared from the sleep that had clouded it.

Cyril had a red mark on the side of his face. Sacha's eyes widened and fear filled him. He'd hit his master. He'd hit his master. He was going to suffer. He was going to be shocked.

Panicked breaths rushed in and out of Sacha's lungs at lightning speed. Tears rolled down his face.

No. No. No. I hurt him. I hit him. I don't want to be hurt.

Cyril gently let go of Sacha as he stopped thrashing. Sacha's hands immediately went to his neck, searching for the collar that would soon shock him. However, he found no collar around his neck nor iron on his ankle.

Right. Cyril didn't like doing that. Not like Master had.

Sacha took a shaky breath. As Cyril walked away, again giving him space he didn't deserve, Sacha stood up.

Carefully, he knelt down at Cyril's side by the door and held out his wrists. He kept his head bowed, trying to be as respectful as possible while asking – no, begging – for punishment.

***

Suddenly, it all clicked for Cyril. Shadow had horrific scarring on his wrists. Whenever he thought he'd done something wrong, he held them out. It wasn't some odd ritual. It was a punishment position.

Cyril felt sick. Shadow had been expecting him to what – cane his wrists bloody? Whip them? Cut them with a knife?

Shadow was absolutely distraught. In all honesty, the punch had startled him, but Cyril had been punched much harder before. It certainly wasn't something that he would hold against Shadow, especially not after a nightmare that had him screaming and thrashing. He would never tell Shadow about it, though.

Cyril found himself overwhelmed. He couldn't just leave. He needed to do something, anything to calm the man down.

Quietly, he knelt down to Shadow's level, took his wrists in his hands to which Shadow flinched, and gently moved them down to his sides.

"Shadow."

To his surprise, Cyril found himself overcome with emotion. He was angry at the way that Shadow had been treated. He was distraught that Shadow thought that he would hurt him. He was sad for the days that Shadow had spent being abused. He was hopeless to get them back for him, too. Most of all, Cyril was confused about why he cared so much.

"I would" – his voice broke a little – "*never*, not in a million years, do that to you."

Shadow looked at him with visible shock in his eyes. Cyril took a shaky breath.

"I've ... " Cyril took another shaky, deep breath and steeled his nerves. "I was a doctor, Shadow. I'm sure you can guess from the supplies and the like, but I was once a doctor. A well paid one, too."

Cyril let go of Shadow's wrists so he wouldn't squeeze them in his anxiety.

"There was – one day, at the hospital I worked at – there was a mass casualty event. I had to give people stitches while they were awake because we didn't have enough rooms to put them all under. We didn't have enough equipment and we needed to save their lives."

A bubble formed in his chest, perhaps an uncried sob, as he continued. "Shadow, I saw true evil that day. I watched someone ... well ... their son ... I watched their son pass away before my very eyes right after *I* had to cause him pain to try to save him from the bleeding. I will ... never forgive myself."

Tears formed in his eyes, but he quickly wiped them away. "Shadow, I will never hurt you. I came out here because I was so scared of becoming like the evil I saw that day that I never wanted to interact with people again. I never wanted to see evil like that. I never wanted to ever risk becoming evil like that, even if I know I don't have it in me."

Shadow looked a little indecisive as Cyril continued talking.

"I understand that you've been seriously hurt. I understand that you don't trust people. I don't trust them either. But please, Shadow, *please*, understand that I will not hurt you."

Cyril pulled Shadow into a tight embrace, holding him close to his body so that Shadow understood that he wouldn't let him get hurt.

"Shadow, everything's going to be okay, whether you believe it or not. I can promise you that, because I will stop at nothing to ensure that everything *will* be okay. Okay?"

He got no response from Shadow, but he didn't know exactly what he was expecting. Instead, Shadow started crying his eerily silent sobs and grabbed his shirt. For once, Cyril was relieved that Shadow felt safe enough to cry instead of begging for a punishment he would not and could not deliver.

"I'll make everything okay if it's the last thing I do, Shadow." Cyril wasn't exactly sure why he was making such a promise, but Cyril was certain that he wasn't just saying it. No, he meant every word of it. He *would* make life better for Shadow. To do anything else just felt wrong.

CHAPTER 10

Thunder crashed overhead.

Never again.

Wind and rain pelted Sacha. His hair, face, and naked body were all soaking wet. He was freezing in the cold northerly winds. His teeth wouldn't stop clattering. Every muscle in his body shivered. His arms hurt from being held around the post in the yard.

The minutes were hours and the hours were days. He wanted to go inside. He wanted to hide. He couldn't take being outside, alone, in the storm anymore.

Again, the whole sky lit up and a loud crash of thunder sounded overhead. From the way the ground rumbled, Sacha knew the lightning had grounded nearby.

I don't want to die like this.

Panic bubbled in his chest. He couldn't make any noise, even if Master wasn't there. Master would surely know if he made any sound.

I don't want to die out here. I can't. I didn't die in the storm before. I can't die in one, tied outside.

Sobs followed the panic. Tears rolled down his face, joining the raindrops that poured from the sky. As he looked around, he realized his gamble was futile. They were in the middle of a forest, in some house, up on a hill. Even if he managed to escape, where would he go? Would he survive the ticks and mosquitos?

Sacha already knew the answer. He wasn't what he once was. He wasn't strong anymore. He'd lost all his muscle, wasting away in that basement. He was probably horribly out of shape, whereas Master seemed to work out every day. Master would always catch him, wouldn't he? He'd catch him and tie him out during every storm to freeze to death.

When Master found Sacha brokenly sobbing outside, he smiled with glee.

"Aww, you look so perfect," he cooed. He brushed the rubble and sticks out of Sacha's hair gently. "So quiet. I should do this more often."

Sacha wanted to beg for Master not to leave him outside again, but he knew better. His silence earned him mercy. Master took him inside from the storm and locked him back in the basement with a dirty towel. That towel might as well have been a gift from the gods.

That wasn't the last time that Master left Sacha outside.

The next time, it was a humid, sweltering night. He was sweating buckets, but couldn't cool off. Heat exhaustion set in quickly.

Again, when Master found him, he cooed gentle mockery into his ear. Sacha was covered in bug bites and ticks.

For once, Master actually took care of them. He removed each tick from Sacha's skin, one by one.

Oh, how Sacha's whole body itched from all the bites. He'd been given uncomfortable punishments before, but nothing like that.

Master came over the next few days, not just to hurt Sacha, but to check on him, too. When Sacha fell ill with horrible chills, fever, and headache after one of his bites had developed a rash, he brought Sacha antibiotics and didn't hurt him for a week.

Sometimes, Master admitted that he'd gone too far. He never said that about that time he was tied outside.

Had Master gone too far, too far to even admit that he did? Or was it intentional? Sacha didn't know. He wasn't sure he wanted to, either.

What he did know was that he didn't see the outside again after that. Master never let him out of the basement, not even to tie him outside.

Somehow, Sacha found comfort in being locked inside. It would be better than the pain of coming back in after being tied outside for so long.

***

Cyril spent a long time in his garden that day. He didn't want to worry Shadow, but he also needed to clear his head and do some thinking. There was no better place for him to do that than his garden.

Pulling weeds was always a good way to let off steam, but he'd already pulled all the weeds out of his garden. He eventually decided to trim his rose bushes, figuring that they were growing a little too wildly and needed their flowers cut back anyway.

He's so afraid of me.

Somehow, being around his flowers always brought Cyril peace. His mind was clearer as he got his pruning shears and went to work on the bushes.

The roses were white, pink, and red. Cyril much preferred white roses, but he could almost hear his mother's voice in his head when he'd picked out the flowers.

It'll look too drab. You need some color in there.

Her favorite had always been pink roses. Red added a good accent with the tulips and peonies.

What would she say to do?

Well, he thought that gaining Shadow's trust would be the most logical place to start. However, that seemed like a Herculean task. Cyril had done everything he could think of to try and gain the poor man's trust.

Share what you love and friendship will follow.

It was something his mother often said. Shadow's biggest problem seemed to be his anxiety and probable post-traumatic stress. It was a catch-22. He needed Shadow's trust in order to help him heal, but the damage that had been done to him was preventing him from trusting.

What had he done, after that day?

I built my garden.

Well, not the next day or even the day after that. It had taken Cyril a couple months to get his savings together, quit his job, and move out to his little cabin in the woods.

Right. I can't rush him.

But I should at least give him a safe place to go so he doesn't feel trapped.

Cyril finally decided to share his garden with someone. The idea of sharing his garden with Shadow was intimidating. It was his private little thinking space, away from the world around him. However, he had a feeling that Shadow needed somewhere like that, too. Even if winter was coming soon and Shadow wouldn't be able to use it, it felt wrong to keep his garden all to himself.

***

"Shadow?"

Sacha perked up from his place beside the hearth and looked intently at Cyril.

"Can I show you something, outside?"

Outside.

Sacha felt panic in his lungs. He was getting punished, wasn't he? He was going to be left out there. Maybe Cyril had seen storms on the horizon and was going to leave him outside. The thought was unbearable.

However, he knew he had to be good. He needed to accept his punishment like a good slave.

As Cyril led him outside and he was blinded by the light pouring out of the sky, the urge to run overwhelmed Sacha. Though he didn't run towards the light. Instead, he sprinted right back to the fireplace.

There were tears in his eyes. He felt like he was freezing.

No.

No. I don't want to be tied outside.

Sacha curled up in a ball and sobbed, knowing that he had defied a direct order.

***

Cyril watched Shadow run into the house with a bit of confusion. He'd merely intended to show Shadow his garden. To see him run off in fear like he'd been shocked confused Cyril.

What the hell did that fucker do to him?

Well, a lot of things was the obvious answer.

One thing about the situation surprised Cyril, though. It was the first time that Shadow had ever directly "disobeyed" him. That running back inside was an instinct – Shadow was scared of the light.

Cyril held back a chuckle at the thought. He was trying to piece together Shadow's actions, after all.

Shadow hadn't worked to repress that instinct.

Could he be becoming more comfortable around me?

The idea that Shadow was perhaps starting to not repress himself as much around Cyril, perhaps subconsciously, warmed Cyril. However, he decided that, like the other times that Shadow was terrified beyond imagination, it would be best to give Shadow his space. There were times for hugs, but this didn't feel like one of them.

Cyril once again began to work on his garden. Was he a tad bit offended that Shadow had run off from his garden? Perhaps, just a bit. It was quite a personal thing for him to share his garden with Shadow.

Cyril reminded himself that it wasn't about him. Shadow was carrying a lot of weight on his shoulders. He was traumatized. He was afraid of everything. Who knew what had happened to make him so afraid of going outside?

The thought left a bitter taste in Cyril's mouth. How had Shadow even gathered the courage to drop dead by his cabin? Was Shadow unwinding because he felt safe or because he couldn't carry the weight of the world on his shoulders anymore?

When Cyril finished his gardening for the day, he came in with fresh cranberries. He'd figured out pretty quickly that Shadow quite liked cranberries. Even if he did his best to suppress his emotions, Cyril was learning the little gestures that meant he was happy, sad, distraught, anything, really.

Shadow was in a crying heap on the floor. His crying was always eerily silent.

Cyril went to Shadow's bed and picked up the weighted blanket. It was another tool from his "Shadow Box" that he'd saved until Shadow had broken down a couple days prior. He wrapped Shadow in it and rubbed his back a bit.

"I'm sorry, Shadow."

Shadow looked up at him with red eyes, before he planted his eyes firmly back on the ground.

"I hope you know that I was just trying to make you feel a bit better." Cyril sighed. "Have some cranberries and go easy on yourself, okay?"

Nothing else really felt appropriate to say.

Shadow looked at him. That little twitch in his eyelid told him that he was nervous and didn't know what to do. Cyril felt awful for taking him outside and being so selfish as to consider his happiness applicable to another.

"I'm going to go make us lunch. Just ... rest. Rest, okay?"

Shadow seemed to do better with orders, even if those orders were confusing.

"Remember what I said. I won't punish you. We all cope differently. My happiness is my garden. Your happiness must be something else and that's okay. Okay?"

He was going to need to make it up to Shadow, somehow. The cranberries were a peace offering for his eventual reconciliation.

What would someone like Shadow enjoy? What would his happiness be? Cyril wasn't quite sure.

"I care for you, Shadow, so please just take care of yourself. You deserve the rest."

Shadow looked at him like "happiness," "rest," and "okay" were words in a completely foreign language. The look shattered Cyril's heart further. Quietly, he turned away and decided to go make lunch, just like he'd said.

Had he really just admitted to Shadow that he cared?

Though it was the truth, to say it aloud was an odd, awkward thing. How long had it been since he said that to someone?

Cyril wasn't sure and he didn't want to think about it too long, lest he be filled with regrets again.

CHAPTER 11

Rain pattered the roof of the cabin. Sadly, it seemed, his fire couldn't survive the rain. He and Cyril had put it out and closed the hatch to protect the fireplace from the downpour.

Of course, that meant that his new Master was there to appraise all of his actions, with nothing more than his weighted blanket to comfort him. Granted, the weighted blanket was like his mother's hugs. Comforting, warm, and relaxing.

However, without the fire in the hearth, Sacha found himself empty. He had nothing to do. He was absolutely useless and if he was useless, it just left more room for Cyril to find a use for him.

Sacha sat by the empty hearth, watching the smoldering coals dance with what remained of their life. Sacha might've felt bad for them, had he not heard a soft noise coming from the opposite wall.

The more Sacha listened, the more he realized that the sound was *mewing*.

Cyril was quick to notice the way that Sacha perked up and looked away from the dying coals.

"What is it, Shadow?"

Sacha froze. Could he tell Cyril? Would Cyril kill the cat if he expressed interest in its life? He knew slaves weren't supposed to have anything they cared about. He didn't want to get the cat hurt for his own selfishness.

Thus, Sacha tried his best to wipe any look of interest off of his face and focus on the coals again.

Cyril made his way over to Sacha and kneeled down to his level. *His* level. He put himself down at Sacha's level. It felt so, so wrong.

"Hey, Shadow, can you look up at me?"

Sacha wouldn't disobey a direct order. He wasn't so stupid. He looked Cyril in the eyes and fought the urge to look away. Sacha didn't want to show his discomfort, lest it be taken advantage of. Or worse, be seen as disobedient or defiant.

"Shadow," Cyril started before he, too, heard the next round of mewling from outside. "Is that a cat?"

Cyril looked at the wall, then at Sacha. Sacha looked at him with fear in his eyes. Cyril was smart. Cyril would figure out that what had interested him was the cat. When Cyril noticed the fear in his eyes, Cyril gave him a look of confusion.

"That's what had your interest." Cyril stood up and swallowed. Sacha's new Master got the familiar apprehension, that nervousness. "I'll be back in soon. I'm going to go check it out."

Cyril got on his rain boots and raincoat, leaving with a towel in hand. When he returned, the mewling was especially loud. The poor little thing looked only a few weeks old – old enough to be off of her mother's milk, but far too young to be on her own. She was a beautiful tortoiseshell with a white muzzle and belly.

Sacha felt a warmth in his heart looking at her. Cyril walked over to Sacha, holding the kitten gently in the towel.

"Can you hold her?"

Sacha nodded dutifully. He would've obeyed any order, much less one so simple. With all the care in the world, Sacha accepted the wet, cold kitten and held her close to his body. He looked down at her with a bit of awe. For a moment, holding her, he could forget about the fear of Cyril killing her before him.

Somehow, despite all instinct, Sacha didn't take Cyril as the type to do that.

Why, he didn't know. But it didn't fit in with the image he had of his new Master in his head.

Cyril returned with a hot water bottle that was just warm, but not too hot. When he turned the corner, he paused, watching the two of them. Sacha was acutely aware of his gaze and tried his best to wipe any emotion off his face.

The fear came next. Tears sprang to his eyes.

"Shadow, it's okay." Cyril approached quietly and handed Sacha the hot water bottle. "Here, put her on the bottle and ... " Cyril went back to the bathroom and returned with a different towel. The new one was much fluffier.

"Here, put her in this, then on the bottle." Cyril simply handed Sacha the towel.

Gently, carefully, like his life depended on it, Sacha wrapped the kitten in the towel and placed her on top of the hot water bottle. Rather quickly, her mewling turned to purring. Sacha's heart warmed again, but he did his best to hide it.

Cyril watched the two of them quietly, from a distance.

"You ... you look happy, Shadow." Cyril sounded shocked.

Sacha's heart dropped.

No. I can't be happy. I can't be happy. I'm not allowed. This isn't right.

Almost as though he read Sacha's thoughts, Cyril continued, "It's okay. It ... it makes me happy to see you happy. Just ... keep being happy."

Sacha almost didn't understand, but he would obey. It was an order, after all. Even if it wasn't right, he still had to obey.

Something in him was growing perhaps the most dangerous emotion a slave could have: doubt. He was beginning to doubt whether or not he'd read Cyril correctly. Was Cyril really cruel? Did he really intend to hurt him?

Of course he did, Sacha told himself.

But if he wanted Sacha to rest in the meantime, before and after that all happened, Sacha could find peace in that.

Just that, on its own, was an impossibly kind mercy from his new owner who watched him tend to the kitten. Sacha couldn't discern the look on Cyril's face at all, but he didn't feel endangered by it.

"We'll keep her."

Sacha turned to Cyril. He couldn't believe what he'd just heard.

Cyril chuckled a bit. Sacha had no idea why. "You keep her company and tend to her, okay? You make sure she's healthy. Show me if she isn't. I think it'll be good for you."

Sacha was in such disbelief that he didn't even notice when Cyril left the room. He immediately felt guilty, but remembered all the times Master had left the room when he was passed out.

It's okay.

Maybe something's going to be okay here.

Sacha, now alone, smiled down at the kitten.

I'll call her Amber.

***

Cyril tried to seem unbothered most of the time. It was easier than growing attached and having to tell people about those parts of his head he didn't want anyone seeing. However, he found it difficult to keep a straight face with Shadow a lot of the time.

Today, he found particularly disturbing. Shadow seemed afraid to express any sort of interest in the kitten outside their house. He seemed afraid when Cyril brought it in. Cyril tried not to take it personally. He knew it wasn't about him. It was a conditioned response taught to him through steel and shocks. However, he couldn't help but be a bit offended that Shadow would think of him as someone who would hurt animals.

Plus, he'd obeyed Cyril's orders like his word was gospel. It was just all-around disturbing.

Something else was bothering him about the interaction, though. He'd noticed during the far too many times he'd seen Shadow naked that Shadow had a number of tattoos along with his scars.

However, it just occurred to him that, like Shadow's brand, he might not have wanted those tattoos. He'd respected Shadow's privacy and hadn't examined them in depth.

He felt stupid for only now thinking of nonconsensual tattoos as a possibility. Cyril suddenly wanted to see them to see if anything could be used to find Shadow again should whoever had kept him go looking for him.

The only problem Cyril ran into was how to approach Shadow about it. He didn't want to scare off Shadow. He didn't want Shadow thinking that he was upset about him having another man's mark on him or whatever horrible other thing Shadow's mind would come up with.

It needed to be done, though. He needed to ensure that they wouldn't have to remove the tattoos to protect Shadow.

After a few hours of letting Shadow care for the kitten, Cyril hoped that he would be calmer.

"Shadow? I need you to do something for me."

Shadow snapped to attention, still careful for the small cat on his lap.

The rain had since stopped and, like clockwork, Shadow had opened the hatch and restarted the fire in the hearth. Cyril smiled a bit before he remembered why he'd left his room.

"Shadow, I ... um ... I noticed that you have tattoos." Cyril was quick to soften the blow. "I don't mind. I mean, I have a lot myself. And it's your right to have control over your own body. But I wanted to look at them. Tattoos can be used to identify people, and I don't want whoever kept you to be able to find you again if they're very identifying."

Shadow looked at him with heartbreaking fear in his eyes. Cyril felt awful. He knew that there was no world in which Shadow would ever not follow a request. Even if he didn't want to do it, Shadow had clearly been trained to ignore what he wanted.

"Just the ones on your chest."

Shadow quietly moved the sleeping kitten over so that she was a safe distance from the fireplace but still close enough to stay warm. He quietly took off his shirt to reveal a body full of scars and some tattoos.

Cyril didn't know whether it would be better to touch Shadow while he looked at the tattoos. Shadow was absolutely petrified. Cyril didn't know what exactly he was afraid of, so he didn't push Shadow by touching him, instead choosing to circle a bit around him so he saw everything.

Many of the tattoos were horribly degrading, but none were overtly meant to identify Shadow as property of anyone else, he thought. The thought that Shadow had endured that made Cyril sick. Still, Cyril did his best to keep it clinical, like he'd done so many times before.

"Shadow, you can put your shirt back on."

Shadow obeyed immediately, making Cyril's stomach twist.

"I – " Cyril swallowed. "I want you to know something, Shadow."

Shadow snapped to attention.

"You can get tattoos faded or removed. If you ever decide that you want some of these tattoos removed or covered or something, we can do that. I have an artist I like. She's really nice. Really good at what she does, too. You'd like her. I'm happy to do that for you, okay? She would be, too."

The admiration and awe in Shadow's eyes caught Cyril off guard.

"Only if you decide to. When you're ready. Okay?"

Shadow was motionless again, but the look in his eyes told Cyril that the prospect made him happy. Thus, Cyril allowed himself to be happy that he'd brought it up.

"Okay. Good. You take care of that kitten, okay? And maybe let me know what you want to name her. She's yours, so you pick her name."

Cyril realized how stupid it all sounded. Shadow couldn't speak. He couldn't let Cyril know what he named the kitten. It just felt wrong to name the kitten for him, though.

Cyril had faith in Shadow. When he was ready, he would find a way to tell him what was on his mind.

He gave Shadow an affectionate touch on the head before he turned to the kitchen. "You keep taking care of her. I'll make us dinner."

CHAPTER 12

Three days after the last day Sacha ever spoke ...

Sacha never thought that he could taste dust. However, locked in a dark room, all alone, dust was about all he could taste. It had been days since he'd had anything to eat, though it was of his own volition. Master had tried to convince him to eat, but food lacked the taste and color it once had. In fact, the world might as well have been just his cage. It would've made no difference. Not even the sky would be blue anymore.

"He won't eat. He won't move. He's just been sitting in that cage for days!"

Master ripped the tarp off of the cage, revealing Sacha's naked, battered form to Master's personal physician. The doctor had to force the look of pure disgust off of his face. Sacha couldn't bring himself to care.

"What the hell have you been doing to him?"

"What do you think?" Master snarled. "Stop fucking questioning me and tell me what the fuck's wrong with him!"

"I don't need to look at him very long to figure out that he's traumatized, sick, and depressed, Emery."

Sacha flinched, remembering all too well what had happened to him when he called Master by his name.

"Sick? Well, give him some medicine, then. What can be done about the rest?"

The doctor looked exasperated and tired. Sacha was amazed that the doctor wasn't hurt for calling Master by his name directly. Then he remembered with a heavy heart that he was a slave. A slave that would never talk again.

"I'll give you some antibiotics to give him, if he'll take them. As for the rest, nothing, Emery. Absolutely nothing. I know you. You wouldn't give him a break to let him recover, even if I told you that's what he needed."

Master growled a bit. "Stop your disrespect. You can be dealt with and I can find another doctor. They're a dime a dozen when you work in my industry. Just have to pay off their student loans."

Master's doctor went quiet, collecting himself. "I would recommend that you let him rest. Give him something to make him feel safe. A blanket or some clothes would be a good place to start."

"The cage is enough. It's his safety."

"*Rest*. He needs rest, desperately. You wanted him quiet and you've gotten that. He can't even move. He's too scared of what you'll do next."

Sacha felt like the doctor was reading his mind, but he couldn't bring himself to care. He'd been violated. His body wasn't his own. He wasn't *Sacha* anymore. He was Master's slave. Nothing else, nothing less. That was his purpose. That was all he was. He didn't deserve rest. He didn't deserve anything nice.

I should just die.

"Hmm ... " Master kneeled down to Sacha's level. Sacha's gaze darted away from him. "So he needs predictability?"

The doctor nodded hesitantly.

"A schedule, then." Master smiled. "I like the idea of making a schedule for him, so he knows exactly what to expect. That way he can prepare himself."

The doctor, behind Master's back, looked exasperated. He had no sympathy for Sacha – that much was clear to Sacha – but if the doctor got Master to let him rest, he would be thankful.

"That would work, yes."

Master nodded. "I'll bring you a clock soon, little Sacha. We'll make a schedule so you know exactly what you'll do each day."

Somehow, knowing ahead of time seemed much worse a torture than not knowing at all. Sacha would've cried, but his tears had dried long ago. Well, perhaps not long ago, but after that night three days ago, he had no more.

***

Sacha didn't know what led him to that closet between Cyril's bedroom and the bathroom. Maybe the living room-kitchen-dining room that had become his home was suddenly too big and too empty. Maybe he remembered that open rooms were never meant to be his safety. Maybe he thought about how he belonged in a cage when he disobeyed.

The day that the cage had gone away, the torments seemed so much more painful. He had nowhere safe to go anymore. Everywhere was dangerous. Everywhere was hell. Nobody would ever understand why a cage was safer than a room. Nevertheless, it made perfect sense to Sacha.

One day, he heard the tight, quiet comfort of the closet calling him. It called louder than any attachment he had to the fire.

Why did it all have to happen to him? Why did he crave that comfort of the only time he'd been given a blanket from Master?

Sacha didn't know. He didn't want to know. He didn't want to have to confront the pain. So, leaving Amber by the fireplace, he took his blankets and hid in the bottom of the closet, wrapping himself tightly.

Time passed differently there. His mind was quiet for once. The memories that plagued him were less ... intense. Though they were more real, it was easier to detach himself when not surrounded by reminders of his own humanity.

There, in the closet, he could find comfort in what he'd been taught. He was a slave. He was for serving and for pleasure. Nobody would be kind to him. That, somehow, was easier to believe than his victimization.

Sacha was still. He felt no hunger, there, in his own mind. He felt no thirst, no will to see little Amber who he'd gotten so attached to. Nothing mattered anyway. Amber deserved better than him. Cyril didn't need him, clearly. He was worthless, useless, and disgusting. Used goods that didn't deserve life.

Tears didn't find him in the closet, not like they did outside. The flashbacks brought numbness. It was a peaceful hell. If his life would always be some form of hell, Sacha certainly preferred the hell he found there, with his weighted blanket, in the closet – alone.

***

Cyril would leave food outside the door for Sacha, but Sacha had decided that he would never leave the closet. He would die there. That would be better than disappointing the Master that had never hurt him time and time again. That would be better than the chance of ever disobeying again.

Sometimes, he would knock on the closet door and tell Sacha things like "I'm worried about you." How could a Master ever be worried about a slave? If he was so worried, why didn't he take Sacha out by the arm and beat him? That was what a slave deserved, after all, if he was truly worrying his Master.

One day, however, Cyril sat outside of the closet.

"Shadow, I'm really, really worried about you. You haven't eaten in three days."

All the better. The fear of being force-fed through a feeding tube was difficult to ignore, but he didn't care what happened to him anymore.

I'm not worthy of your food. He was worthless. He did nothing for Cyril. He had no clue why Cyril cared so much for such a useless slave. If he wasn't serving his Master, he didn't deserve food.

"Can you come out, please? I know you're probably going through a lot right now and I understand that you probably don't want to see me, but you need to eat."

Just drag me out. I can't do the impossible.

It was an order.

An order that Sacha decided to disobey. Some part of him missed the pain. He wanted to be shown his place forcefully. He wanted someone to hurt him. That was his normal. He wanted his normal back. It was also his life. He wanted his life back, too.

How selfish of him.

Instead of pulling him out of the closet, Cyril merely stood up and walked away with a sigh.

A darker, more sinister thought lingered in his mind. He was right next to Cyril's bedroom. Had his coaxing been an order to enter?

Suddenly, Sacha realized that he'd made himself completely unavailable to Cyril. That was the one thing a slave could never be – unavailable. He'd manipulated Cyril into feeling bad for him. He was a bad person. Cyril had wanted him and he'd denied Cyril that.

It felt like marching to his death to walk into Cyril's bedroom. Sacha didn't know if he'd prefer his clothes to be taken off ahead of time or if he preferred to strip Sacha himself. Master had never let him wear clothes, really, so it was never an issue before. Now, Cyril gave him clothes. What was he meant to do with them?

Sacha looked around and realized that Cyril didn't have cuffs or anything of the sort to tie him down with during the act. Would he expect Sacha to lie there and accept it? Without restraints? Sacha wasn't sure he could do that.

Cyril always kept a length of rope in his storage cabinet near the front. Sacha decided to go get it and beg for Cyril to tie him down.

Sacha sat there quietly, obediently, kneeled next to the bed. When rustling came from the door and he saw Cyril, his heart skipped a beat. He wasn't ready for such an intimate betrayal.

"Shadow ... ?"

Sacha bowed his head and offered out the length of rope. He hoped that Cyril would be gentle and use lube. He hoped that Cyril would be quick in taking his pleasure. He hoped that he would be enough for Cyril.

"Shadow, what's ... "

Sacha squeezed his eyes closed, pushing the rope out more with his scarred hands and wrists. *Please. Please just take me. Take your pleasure. Let me be useful, please.*

Sacha wanted to be useful. He wanted his normal back. He'd do anything at all to have some semblance of what he knew back then. He wanted to rip his skin off for Cyril to prove his loyalty and commitment. He wanted to show Cyril how much it hurt him *not* to be hurt.

Sacha didn't understand. He needed Cyril to make him understand. Sex felt like the way that Cyril would want to do it.

Chapter 13

The last day Sacha ever spoke

Sacha knew it would happen eventually. Master had taken him by the wrist and dragged him up into his bedroom, fresh bruises still forming from the day of torture he'd just faced.

Walking up the two flights of stairs with his arms bound behind his back was like walking up to the gallows for an execution. Sacha had long since lost his will to fight. In fact, once he realized that Master would rape him that night, he could only shrivel up inside and wish that he'd find the means to die the next day.

Master's bed was huge and luxurious. Thick, warm blankets and expensive pillows lined it all. However, most noticeably, chains were readied at the headboard and foot of the bed.

Sacha felt tears well in his eyes as he froze, staring at the bed.

"Get up, slave."

Sacha didn't comply. He couldn't.

Master hit the button on his shock collar, sending Sacha to the floor in awful, seizing pain. Keeping his hands tied behind his back was intentional, Sacha realized. It was to keep him from clawing his neck.

Once the convulsing pain stopped, Master picked him up by the hair. "You will be shocked until you get on the bed, little slave."

Sacha couldn't recover in time before the next wave of electrifying pain took him over. He couldn't help it – he screamed. Master stopped the shocks almost immediately and took him by the neck.

Squeezing his throat, he looked Sacha in the eyes. "Don't you fucking dare make a noise. I told you I want you silent at all times. That includes here."

Master dropped him and Sacha hit the floor with an agonizing *thump* as he landed directly, perhaps intentionally, on his wrecked shoulder and ankle from the past days' torture sessions. He forced himself to hold back a whimper.

"Now, on the bed."

It was impossible, but Sacha had long realized that he had to do the impossible for Master. Struggling to his feet, he wasn't fast enough for Master. He fell to the ground with another horrible wave of shocks. Tears formed in his eyes.

Master seemed to tire of the game and instead pulled Sacha onto the bed by his bad arm. Sacha panicked. He couldn't breathe, not over the pain, not over what would happen. Master quietly, angrily removed the cuffs and attached his arms overhead.

"Please don't do this, Master. Please. I can't do this."

A sharp backhand silenced his pleas. "Silence," Master hissed.

Sacha already had bruises on his jaw that were growing visibly from the amount of times Master had hit him.

Master took his time securing Sacha's naked form to the bed, ensuring he would not be able to escape. It dawned on Sacha, though not for the first time, that he had no choice in the matter. As Master secured a gag in his mouth, tears found Sacha easily.

"There. Now you'll be nice and quiet." Master smiled a bit down at him. "Don't worry. This doesn't have to be all bad, hmm?"

Of course it will be. How could I ever enjoy this?

Master took his sweet time stroking Sacha's cock and massaging inside him with lube. It took everything in him to stay quiet. He wanted to fight. He wanted to push Master off of him. He wanted Master to get his hands off of him. To his horror, he was growing hard under Master's ministrations. He wanted it all to stop, but couldn't even cry out a plea.

With a wolfish grin, Master slipped out of his trousers. He jerked himself a little, looking at Sacha's horribly bruised and battered body. Master took Sacha's cock in his hand and planted a small kiss on it. Sacha forced himself to hold back a sob. He hated how hot and needy he felt. He wanted it all to stop.

"You're gorgeous. I don't know how much longer I can wait," he said with a chuckle.

No. No. Please stop.

The answer was not much longer. Within minutes, Master checked that he was ready and pushed past the ring of tight muscle. Sacha screamed, feeling like he was going to be split in half.

A sharp slap to the face broke his lip this time. "Come on. It isn't that bad. Or is my cock really that thick?"

Master was gleeful as he thrust into Sacha, placing himself deep into him and holding himself there. A heavy moan escaped Master's mouth.

"You feel so good."

Sacha thought he was going to die as Master began to move, thrusting hard and fast in and out of him. At one point, Sacha felt a faint popping sensation, then a coolness that was quickly followed by burning, searing hot pain. He realized that he was bleeding from the unbearably painful thrusting of his Master.

Tears fell onto the deaf ears of his Master. Yet all that Sacha could hear was the sound of Master moaning and forcing Sacha to come. He couldn't stay present. In fact, he didn't even feel alive. As Master fucked him, a part of him really did die.

Nobody could know that Master had done this to him. Nobody would ever understand the depth of the pain. As Master's seed filled him and a horrible squelch filled the room, Sacha vowed to never talk again. His body was a traitor. He had nothing.

Sacha's tears dried as Master stroked his thighs and told him how good he was. How he was made for being fucked. That last holdout inside him broke. He no longer even had the will to move.

The last sound Sacha ever made was a faint whimper before he retreated completely into his own head, the only place where he was truly safe.

***

Suddenly, everything clicked into place for Cyril. The scars around his ankles and wrists from cuffs, the tattoos, the brand, the reactions, the fear of his bedroom. Cyril felt ill. Whoever kept Shadow before him had raped him. More than once from the horrible way Shadow kneeled at his bedside, holding the rope out for him.

Shock froze Cyril in place. God, what was he supposed to do? How could he ever convince Shadow that he didn't want that from him? He had never had any interest in sex, much less hurting someone in the process.

"Shadow," Cyril tried to keep his voice measured, to keep the shake out of it, but completely and utterly failed. "Did whoever kept you before rape you?"

Cyril felt he already knew the answer, but he wanted to confirm in case he was jumping to conclusions.

Shadow was still with tears in his eyes. He was frozen, in fact, with paralyzing fear.

"Shadow, I really need you to answer me. Just nod if yes, shake your head if no."

Shadow was still for a while longer. Then, for the first time, he nodded his head. Tears spilled out from his eyes soon after. Shadow couldn't control his sobbing.

"Is ... this the first time you've ever admitted or told anyone that that happened to you, Shadow?"

Again, Shadow nodded, though with less hesitation the second time. For the first time, Cyril saw just how worn down and broken Shadow was. As he curled up into a ball, holding onto the rope like a lifeline, sobbing audibly, Cyril had no clue what to do.

"I'm so ... so ... so ... sorry." Cyril took a seat next to Shadow, rubbing his back as he cried into his knees. He'd never been the person of such trust before and Cyril wasn't sure how to handle it.

"I believe you, Shadow. I believe you. It must've been awful. Nobody should have to go through that."

Shadow just kept sobbing and sobbing, like all the tears he never cried were coming out all at once. Cyril tried to think about what else he could say to Shadow to make it better, but realized that nothing he could say would ever undo the pain of what he'd gone through.

"Shadow, I would never do that to you." Cyril tried to find the words he needed for a while, before he was ready to speak again. "I've never had an interest in people ... like that. I've never enjoyed sex. I would never, ever do that to you. There's nothing interesting about sex to me, much less what you were put through."

Cyril swallowed a bit. "What you went through ... that wasn't normal. That wasn't right. You deserve so much better than that. I know you're in a lot of pain because of it right now and that's okay."

Their cat came strutting into the room to investigate, then began to swipe at Shadow's leg. Cyril got ready to remove the cat and put her back outside the bedroom, but was stopped by Shadow unwinding from his ball and pushing his back against the bed. He picked up the small kitten and began to pet her very gently.

Cyril, for the first time, saw a glimpse of who Shadow might've been beyond all the trauma. He was a gentle soul, that much was obvious. Maybe he would've been a veterinarian or an animal rescuer. Perhaps even a nurse or a doctor. He had the healing instinct, Cyril could tell.

His own healer's instinct took over for a moment. He wanted to help Shadow become that gentle person who cared for an orphaned kitten with all the care in the world again. He wanted Shadow to be happy. He'd gone this far. Shadow had trusted him enough to admit that he'd been a victim of repeated, violent rapes. Cyril owed him as much for having that much trust in him.

"Shadow, is it okay to hug you?"

Shadow hesitated, but eventually nodded. Cyril pulled him into a tight hug, careful of the kitten.

"One day, Shadow, whether you believe it or not, this will all be behind you." Cyril stroked Shadow's hair gently. "One day, you'll find your happiness. With me, you have nothing to be scared of. Okay?"

Shadow was still, finally calming in his arms. He still cried, but Cyril had a suspicion that the tears were from relief.

"I'm not perfect. I'm not a mind reader. But we'll work together so that you can be happy here or wherever you end up. I can promise you that much. I won't give up. I promise that, too."

Shadow looked at him with a look in his eyes that Cyril couldn't quite place at first. Was it hope? Was it disbelief? Could someone like Shadow even understand what that meant after what must've been years of trauma?

Cyril's heart hurt for Shadow. Whatever he could do, he would do. He wasn't a superhero. He didn't have magic. He was only human and a flawed one at that. But, in his heart of hearts, he promised himself that Shadow would be happy if it was the last thing he did.

Cyril pulled Shadow further into his hug, before he let him go.

"Everything's going to be okay, eventually, Shadow. I promise you that."

Somehow, Shadow looked like he might have believed it.

Chapter 14

The truth of the matter hit Sacha like a bag of rocks.

Cyril had never been mad at him. Cyril hadn't even requested to use him. Cyril had just been genuinely concerned for Sacha's wellbeing.

His promises of happiness were a bit too kind for a slave – one who shouldn't have desires other than to please – but Sacha found something that tasted like reassurance in them.

More than anything, though, he wanted to shrivel up and die. That day when Master had used him the first time, he'd vowed never to tell anyone. Yet, here he was, telling someone. Master hadn't even allowed small nods of his head, so Sacha figured that nodding was as close to telling as he'd ever get.

He was embarrassed. He'd let such a horrible thing happen. He thought nobody would ever believe him. Yet that was the first thing that Cyril had said to him. How was he supposed to react? What was the correct thing to do?

His shame was so deep and all-consuming. Could he ever really share that part of himself as a victim, like Cyril seemed to believe? Could he ever be brave enough to explore the idea that what Master had done was something *other* than his purpose as a slave? To see what those emotions he'd buried in a grave long ago held?

Would everything ever be okay? Maybe. Maybe he could be okay if his new Master didn't want to be serviced. Oh, he would take any punishment, any torture, if it meant not having to be spread open on a bed again. If somebody believed him about what he'd gone through, maybe he could believe it, too.

The ringing in his ears was getting particularly loud. It was always there, but got worse when he was stressed. When did that start? Was that before or after his first time with Master? Surely it was the result of a punishment that he'd earned. Maybe it had been intentional.

He squeezed his eyes shut at the thought of the punishments that came when he didn't service Master correctly.

There was something else there – something that tasted vaguely like relief. Not necessarily relief that he wasn't going to be forced to service Cyril or that he wasn't going to be punished for making Cyril upset, but a confusing, strange relief he couldn't quite pinpoint the origin of.

Was he relieved to not have to act like a slave? To not have to bottle up his emotions?

He quickly put the thought aside. Of course not. He was a slave and he would be a good one. Whatever that meant to Cyril.

Did he believe Cyril? Was it wrong to believe it was all trickery? Sacha didn't know the answer to those questions. Master might've told him that he was perceptive, but Cyril wasn't like Master at all. Would he be offended? Sacha thought so.

However, he couldn't bring himself to obey and believe Cyril.

For that, he knew he deserved punishment.

Sacha held back tears, knowing that punishment, that normalcy, would never be his again. No, he was not relieved to not be punished. He needed correction. It was only right.

Nevertheless, he allowed himself a moment of comfort in the idea of being corrected without being in pain.

***

Cyril thought for many hours after "the incident" about how to confront Shadow without scaring him. He was beginning to realize that Shadow needed some sort of structure – more than he was currently providing.

Something felt wrong about assigning Shadow a schedule of things to do. Even if he needed more structure to know that he hadn't done anything wrong, maybe keep the anxiety away, Cyril felt like having Shadow do chores around the cabin would be taking advantage of his vulnerability.

Yet, if Shadow wanted to do something like that, who was he to deny Shadow that? Shadow was a person. He could make decisions for himself.

Cyril let out a frustrated sigh and wiped the sweat off of his forehead. Shadow was vulnerable. He would do anything Cyril asked him, clearly. So, how could he know that, if he gave Shadow a schedule of chores, Shadow would listen of his own volition and not obligation?

It was a question that probably had no answer. Shadow was conditioned to act a certain way and believe certain things about himself, clearly. The line between his free will and his conditioning was perhaps blurry at best.

Cyril finally emerged from his garden to Shadow watching the fire with interest. He was still wrapped in the weighted blanket, just the way that Cyril had left him after the incident. Something about him felt calmer with that blanket.

The idea of ruining Shadow's small moment of peace with a topic that would clearly scare him upset Cyril. He knew he needed to do it, but bringing himself to do it was difficult.

"Shadow?"

Shadow snapped to attention in that horrible, obedient way.

"I need to talk to you."

Shadow stood up quickly, dropping the blanket on the floor. Cyril was quick to motion for him to sit back down. He couldn't ever convince Shadow to sit in a chair, so Cyril joined him on the floor and wrapped him back up in his weighted blanket.

"I promise that I'm not angry with you for earlier." Cyril took a deep breath, saying the words he'd rehearsed in his head. "If ever I seem angry, it's because I'm mad at the person who did that to you. Not you, Shadow. Never you."

Shadow looked at him with anxious apprehension.

"I know you're probably struggling because you don't know what to expect. So, I thought I'd tell you. I ... um ... " Cyril gave an anxious glance around the room. "For one, nothing sexual. If someone tries to do something like that to you, find some way to tell me, okay? Because that isn't right and it won't happen if I have something to do with it."

Cyril motioned to the room around them. "This here, this is all safe. I have no intentions of hurting you. I want you to recover and then, well, I want you to be able to go somewhere else and do something in safety. I don't know how possible that is, but that's my goal. You don't need to do anything in return. Chores, anything like that. You don't need to do that."

Cyril waited quietly, anxiously, for Shadow to respond, but soon realized that he couldn't. He tried to read Shadow's body language, but, besides the overwhelming anxiety that always plagued Shadow, Cyril couldn't decipher anything in particular. If anything, Shadow seemed anxious, but ambivalent.

Could he be relieved? Definitely not. There wasn't any way that Shadow could be ambivalent. It was a trained response, Cyril was sure. However, he soon realized he was helpless to change it. That would be up to Shadow, when he felt safer.

Though the situation was frustrating, Cyril recognized that it somehow represented significant progress. At least Shadow was calm.

Cyril had a feeling that if they'd had that conversation a couple weeks ago, Shadow would've broken down into a panic attack.

Yes, his ambivalence was, indeed, some twisted form of progress.

For that, Cyril allowed himself to feel proud – both of Shadow and of himself.

"We'll work on being able to make decisions again, okay? We'll work on you choosing what you want to do, instead of what ... you must think I want you to do, okay? It'll get better, eventually. You'll be able to tell me 'no,' one day, I'm sure."

Somehow, Cyril felt like he was making a promise he couldn't keep. That feeling only made him more determined to end up keeping it.

***

Sacha watched Cyril in the kitchen cautiously, still mulling over what Cyril had told him. He'd fully expected to be punished, not to be gently ... was scolded the word? Perhaps it was, perhaps it wasn't. It didn't feel like a scolding, not the way that Master had scolded him.

Scolding perhaps meant that he would feel small and powerless. With Cyril, he'd almost felt the opposite. Cyril had talked about saying no and making decisions for himself.

That wasn't what a slave was meant to do.

Decisions were for his Master to make. They weren't his. He couldn't tell anyone no. That wasn't his place.

It was all so confusing that he wanted to cry.

However, Sacha found quickly that he wouldn't really need to. Cyril walked over with a mug full of hot chocolate, freshly made with the whole milk he got from ... somewhere.

Where does he get his milk?

It wasn't Sacha's place to ask.

"I'm not hungry after everything and I guessed you weren't either, but I wanted to make you something before I head back outside."

Sacha accepted the hot chocolate because it was what Cyril wanted him to do. He drank a bit of it hesitantly, but found it only to be pleasantly warm. He could've breathed a sigh of relief. He wouldn't have to drink something scalding hot.

Sacha almost thought that Cyril would stay and make sure he was appreciative of the gift. However, what he'd said before, combined with the quiet way he picked up the weighted blanket Sacha had left on the floor, told him otherwise.

Cyril wrapped Sacha tightly in it, ruffling his hair a little. Then he left out the door.

Sacha felt as empty as the room, a hearth without a fire. Some part of him wished that Cyril had stayed. Some deep, buried part of himself almost wished he could call Cyril back.

***

"Shadow, can you come here?"

Cyril's cabin had few windows. Cyril preferred it that way. The privacy of not having anyone peeking into his quarters was reassuring, especially now that he had such traumatized, injured company with him. He also lived very far away from any cities. Again, he preferred it that way. The town had everything he needed.

Shadow walked over to him.

One of the other good things about living far from the city was the sky. Cyril had wanted to show Shadow the sky, but ever since he'd run in from outside having a panic attack, Cyril had second-guessed himself.

In his garden, looking through the window in the side door to the kitchen, Cyril realized that he didn't need to take Shadow outside for him to see the stars.

Cyril motioned for Shadow to stand by the door.

"Let me get the lights."

Shadow nodded.

Once all the lights except the fire in the hearth were extinguished, the sight outside the window became clear.

A cloud of stardust had covered the night sky in a wave, like sand through a current. Millions of stars twinkled above them, dancing through the sky, singing stories of worlds far away. Cyril always felt awe when looking at such a magnificent sight. It never got old or normal.

He smiled a bit when he looked at Shadow. Shadow, for a moment, looked happy. Nostalgic, maybe.

Has he seen something like this before?

Cyril realized he knew nothing about Shadow other than his trauma. Surely Shadow had a life before what had happened to him. What was that life like? What did he do? Did he have family? Someone he loved? Did he go to school?

The idea made Cyril's heart hurt. All that would have been stripped away. Even if his life hadn't been good before his captivity, surely it was better than the constant torture Shadow must've endured.

Cyril wanted to know. If it was good, he wanted Shadow to be able to return to that. If it wasn't good, then he wanted to help Shadow build a new life for himself. Maybe, even if it was good, he wouldn't want to return to it and want to build a new life. That would be fine, too.

Determination filled Cyril. Shadow would have a life beyond his cabin. Shadow would be able to build a new life or return to his old one. Cyril would make sure it was a good life, too.

CHAPTER 15

Tears rolled down Sacha's cheek as he looked out at the stars. How long had it been since he'd seen them?

It took him back to all those sleepless nights he'd spent setting traps on the water with the other young sailors from the town. He'd always been particularly good at the sails. The most beautiful nights for the stars, though, they always relied on their motors. After all, wind and clouds were never one without the other.

Did it make him happy to see the stars again? Was he happy to know that he still remembered his life before Master?

Would he ever return to that quiet life, out on the water? Would it ever be the same after the storm that had landed him with Master?

Sacha didn't know the answer to those questions. Somehow, he felt he didn't want to know them quite yet, either. Just thinking about the past few years was overwhelming enough without having to think about the years of what he'd left behind.

That night, Sacha gazed empty-hearted at the fire. When Cyril left the room, he remembered just how truly alone he was. Even if Cyril was his Master and owned his life, his company was better than nothing.

After all, his family thought he was dead. Master had shown him his obituary and pictures of his headstone. He could never return to them, could he?

No, he would never put his family through that pain. He'd caused people enough pain already.

They would have to see what he'd become – a useless, submissive slave, a shell of his former self. He couldn't bear the shame. He couldn't stand the helplessness as they looked at him, surely horrified by what he'd become. Surely, they would abandon him. That was a pain he knew he couldn't handle.

***

Eventually, everything was routine again. Cyril didn't bring the incident back up to Sacha. In fact, to Sacha's shock and dismay, Cyril seemed to let it all completely slide.

It felt so beyond wrong. Sacha had overstepped his place. He'd done something *wrong* and *offensive*. He should've been punished by Cyril – locked somewhere dark, not allowed to see even so much as a ray of sunlight.

Sacha almost went back into the closet, but his fear of doing the wrong thing with the new, strange rules that Cyril had given him was overwhelming. Sacha wanted to do the right thing. He wanted to do well. He just didn't know what that would look like to Cyril. Healing? *Making decisions*? That wasn't his place. That wasn't what he was supposed to do. But if it was what Cyril wanted as his new Master, what did it matter? If he didn't follow his orders, he would be punished.

The fear of not knowing what to do drove Sacha to do anything he could to be useful, so that Cyril would have a reason to keep him.

Even if Cyril was a Master with strange rules and even stranger expectations, he hadn't yet hurt Sacha. Even if the absence of pain was stressful, Sacha didn't want to be killed. That was what happened to useless slaves, after all. Useless, disobedient slaves didn't deserve life and Sacha felt more useless and disobedient than ever.

As awful as it felt to admit, he also didn't want to go back to Master, not when Cyril was so kind. He couldn't have wants – he knew that. But if he could have one thing, it would be to not go back to Master. He didn't care if Cyril would sell him once he was healed – something told Sacha that Cyril would find him someone kinder than Master.

For that to happen, though, Sacha knew he had to prove his usefulness. His body constantly ached, despite being the most healed he'd been in years. Most days, he found little strength to do anything. Yet he knew he had to.

Cyril always made lunch. Making food was simple and if he did it well, he could be rewarded well in return, right?

The task proved more difficult than it seemed. The dizziness hit not even five minutes into chopping carrots.

His vision hadn't been the same since he met Master, either. The colors of the world were duller. It was as though a white, blurry film covered everything, like seeing the world through wax paper. He could hardly see three feet in front of himself, too.

It wasn't really a problem when viewing the bright light of the fireplace. However, when combined with the dizziness, it made moving things around and cooking more difficult than he'd expected.

Sacha thought that despite the difficulty, he was holding it together well. He was doing his job well. He was going to make soup and Cyril was going to see that he was useful. That was, until he missed the table.

Just as the door opened, hot soup went clattering down to the ground with a loud, metal *twang*.

Sacha could hardly believe his eyes.

Immediately, tears rolled down his face. He couldn't breathe. He'd dropped something. He'd wasted food. Food was worth more than him. He was worthless for dropping it. He'd never be forgiven for wasting so much soup.

Cyril was over by him in an instant. He checked Sacha over with undeserved kindness. "Did you get burned?"

Without thinking, Sacha whimpered. *No. No. I can't make noise. I was already too loud.*

"It's okay, Shadow. Deep breaths."

How could he take deep breaths when he couldn't breathe?

"Shadow, look at me."

Sacha couldn't meet Cyril's gaze.

"Shadow."

Sacha knew that tone. He was doing something wrong, wasn't he? God, he was so useless. He was going to be sent away.

"Shadow, really, it's okay. Are you burned?"

Sacha shook his head a little, staring down at the mess on the floor. He was awful.

Cyril put a light hand on his shoulder, which made Sacha flinch away a few feet. Immediately, his hands went to his face. He curled to protect his ribs.

Cyril merely sighed and motioned instead.

"Let's get you to your spot."

Gently, Cyril led Sacha over to his spot by the fireplace. Tears overwhelmed Sacha's vision. He didn't want to be punished. He even flinched when Cyril wrapped him in his weighted blanket. Cyril seemed annoyed. Was he really going to be punished? After all the promises?

Sacha should've known better. Promises were empty words.

***

Cyril didn't punish Sacha.

After he was done cleaning up Sacha's mess while Sacha was a useless, crying mess on the floor next to the fireplace, Cyril tried to convince Sacha to eat. Sacha refused. He knew it meant that he could be force-fed later, but Sacha didn't care. He wasn't worthy of food. He should've been starved.

Cyril ate a piece of bread with some meat, far worse than the meal that Sacha had prepared. If only he hadn't screwed up, his Master might've eaten something better than meat and bread. God, he was so useless.

A sick thought occurred to Sacha.

Maybe Cyril was testing him and his usefulness. Maybe Cyril wanted to see that Sacha knew his place as a slave.

Master had sometimes done such a thing. He'd promise Sacha punishment, then leave him alone for days in that awful cage. Sacha would eventually be driven to punish himself in any way he could – whether it was starving himself or directly injuring himself. Master was always pleased. Master had known that he was loyal that way.

Sacha looked over at the fire. The coals were burning hot in the hearth. He dreaded burning more than most other types of punishment. The wounds never healed well. The skin would always flake away and peel in agonizing ways, leaving blisters and pus to leak out.

It would make for a good way to prove his loyalty to Cyril.

Even if Sacha knew it was the right thing to do, even if he knew it could be what Cyril wanted, he couldn't bring himself to do it. The coals would burn so badly. He would need to hold them for a few seconds, of course. They'd sear the inside of his palm. Doing work would be so very painful, but that was what he deserved for being so useless.

How could anyone bring themself to burn their own hand with hot coals? Sacha knew that it didn't matter. He was a slave, capable of the normally impossible. If it was what his Master wanted, he had to do it, no matter how painful it was.

Still, he sat there and stared as the glare of the sun left the windows. Cyril always stayed out until a little after sundown, especially with the days getting shorter.

Sacha had to do it.

He had to burn himself.

He had to do the impossible.

With the poker, Sacha moved one coal towards him. He picked one from the center of the fire so it would be especially hot. Even just sitting there, it was glowing, shining red and orange, dancing with heat.

Sacha closed his eyes and picked it up with his hand. Immediately, it began to sear his hand. The smell of burning flesh filled the room. Sacha couldn't help it. He screamed.

The door slammed open the next moment. Sacha dared to look at Cyril's panicked face, running towards him and his coal.

"Shadow? Shadow, what were you thinking?!"

Sacha dropped the coal without a second thought.

Cyril grabbed Sacha's hand, which made Sacha whimper. Cyril immediately dragged Sacha over to the sink, running cold water over his burn.

For once, the normally calm Cyril looked furious. The look of fury quickly went away, but the horrible look on his face was burned into Sacha's mind.

Had he not done the right thing?

He'd punished himself. That was what Cyril wanted, right?

Sacha whimpered from the pressure on his wrist. He was hyperventilating. He couldn't think. Tears were pouring from his eyes.

It took him a moment to realize that Cyril was similarly panicking.

"Shadow, what was that?"

The tone in Cyril's voice pushed Sacha further into his shell. He squeezed his eyes shut, the burn on his hand only beginning to feel marginally better.

Please have mercy. I'm so sorry.

"Shadow, why did you do that? Did you want to hurt yourself?"

Sacha shook his head furiously. He'd never wanted to do that. It was what he thought Cyril wanted.

"Did you think I wanted that or something?"

Sacha nodded a bit, hanging his head in shame.

Cyril thumbed his nose bridge, closing his eyes and holding Sacha's hand steady under the water.

"Let's pray that this isn't too bad of a burn. The last place I want to go is the hospital."

Cyril stood there. Sacha could feel the rage radiating off of him. It scared him more than when Master had gotten mad. Cyril was kind. He didn't normally hurt Sacha. He hadn't even gotten mad at Sacha for screaming, even if he knew he shouldn't have done that.

Through the hiccuping sobs and the pain that was making him dizzy, Sacha just kept repeating apologies to himself, as though it would calm his panic attack.

I'm sorry. I'm sorry. I'm sorry. "I'm sorry."

Sacha didn't realize until the grip on his hand let go.

The shock on Cyril's face was horrible. It made him want to hide.

"What?"

He'd apologized. Out loud.

CHAPTER 16

Cyril wasn't having a good day. Apparently, Shadow wasn't, either.

First, the dropped soup and the subsequent panic attack from Shadow. Cyril didn't want to imagine what would've happened to him had he dropped the soup and *not* been with him. Shadow had refused to eat. It broke Cyril's heart.

Did he think himself unworthy of food? Cyril's own helplessness and incompetence haunted him while he was in his garden afterwards. He had planned to stay out there, staving off memories of a much worse time, until he heard the scream.

Shadow never made noise.

Shadow never talked.

Yet he'd done both in the span of a few minutes.

Cyril didn't know what to think or say.

The panic was immediate. Shadow ran like a cornered animal, darting into the closet where Cyril had found him before.

He needed to be calm. He needed to hold it together, no matter how shocked he was. He could hear, actually *hear*, Shadow's broken sobbing from the closet. Cyril knew that sound well. It was the sound of a man who had nothing left to lose.

What had happened to make talking so terrifying? That was another thing that Cyril didn't want to even guess.

Soon enough, Cyril was hearing dry heaving along with the tears. His heart shattered.

"Shadow?"

Cyril approached the closet door, leaving it shut between them. He figured that maybe, if there was a physical barrier, that Shadow would feel more comfortable.

Shadow just groaned miserably and went back to crying.

"Shadow, honey, I'm not mad at you."

The crying paused momentarily. Cyril's heart sang with hope.

"Shadow, listen to me for a minute, okay?" Cyril took a deep breath. "I'm not angry at you. In fact, if anything, I'm happy."

***

Sacha looked at the door, protected momentarily from the rage of his Master. What in the world did Cyril mean? How could he be happy? Sacha had broken the most important rule for a slave like him – be seen, but not be heard.

Master – not Master, Cyril – Cyril was angry at him.

"What?"

Master was standing in front of him. Sacha had been good. He hadn't slipped up in a while. Yet, somehow, he'd let out a small "sorry."

"What the hell did you say? Did you apologize?"

A sharp backhand sent Sacha to the floor. His head was already pounding from what he could only guess was a concussion and the impact made him black out.

Cyril's voice brought him out of his flashback.

"Shadow, I was worried about you. I'm not angry at you. I promise. You have a lovely voice. I didn't know you could talk. I thought it was possible that something had happened to you that rendered you unable to speak."

He heard Cyril take another deep breath. Why would he be breathing like that if he wasn't angry?

"You went through a lot. I'm shocked you can talk at all." Cyril's voice began to break a bit. "This is about you, but it breaks my heart to think that somebody – " He paused. "Somebody out there taught you that you couldn't use your voice and couldn't make noise."

Sacha stared at the door, dumbfounded. Why was Cyril getting emotional? Wasn't it normal for slaves not to talk? For a moment, his tears dried. He couldn't process what Cyril was saying. He was just too stupid, really.

"Can you come out, Shadow, honey?"

It was an order, no matter how nicely it was said. The door was protection, but Cyril didn't want him to have it.

Slowly, but surely, Sacha opened the door to see Cyril with tears in his eyes, smiling at him. Again, Sacha was struck with overwhelming confusion. Why was Cyril smiling? Why was he crying?

Had Sacha done something right? Had he really made his Master happy? Did talking make Cyril happy, not angry?

Didn't he deserve punishment? For breaking that one rule twice in the same day?

"Shadow, I understand that talking terrifies you."

Tears formed in Sacha's eyes. He couldn't take the confusion. He didn't understand.

"I want you to keep talking, slowly. At your own pace. Like I said, you really have a lovely voice. You should use it more."

An order. One directly contradicting everything he'd known before. New tears filled Sacha's eyes. He couldn't help himself. He broke down sobbing.

He wasn't going to be punished. He wasn't going to be forced into silence anymore. Sacha didn't know how to feel. He didn't know what to think. But the taste in his mouth tasted something like relief.

"Can I give you a hug, Shadow?"

Sacha nodded a bit. Gently, Cyril wrapped his arms around Sacha and, as Sacha broke down crying at the gentle, human touch he was so unused to, Cyril began to rock him a bit.

"I'm so sorry that all of this happened to you, Shadow. You didn't deserve it. You didn't deserve any of it."

Sacha found himself gripping onto Cyril's shirt a bit. He couldn't think, so he didn't. He was a slave, after all. It wasn't his place to think and make decisions. It wasn't his place to have opinions on orders, even if they felt totally wrong.

Though, something occurred to Sacha, a thought that seemed almost illogical.

If Cyril wasn't going to punish him for overstepping his place, disobeying orders, hurting himself, or talking, what would he punish him for?

Something in Sacha, some instinct he'd long since buried, seemed to tell him that the answer was nothing at all. Cyril might not want him punished for anything. That thought only made him cry harder into Cyril as he rocked Sacha gently. The gentle, human touch that came whenever he panicked and cried might be the replacement for painful, horrible punishments.

It seemed like an impossible mercy. It couldn't be true.

Could it?

***

Cyril hugged Shadow's crying form long into the night. At one point, he'd started crying, too, but at what point he'd started or stopped, he didn't know.

He was rarely so emotional as to cry. However, when he heard Shadow talk, then cry, then trust him enough to come out of hiding, it was hard not to. He'd worked so hard with Shadow. He'd done so much to gain his trust with failure after failure. *Finally*, after all his attempts to get Shadow to trust him, at least subconsciously, Shadow had trusted him enough to talk, to apologize, to come out the closet.

When had he gotten so attached? Cyril guessed it was somewhere between bringing Shadow back from the verge of death and the first time he'd cried in his arms.

As a doctor, Cyril had gotten used to not getting attached to his patients, especially in the emergency room. Not everyone was going to make it, after all. He was there for a brief period in their lives – an important one, sure, but still only a few hours out of the thousands of a lifetime. He almost preferred it that way a lot of the time. Cyril wasn't sure he could handle dealing with patients who refused to comply with treatment time and time again over years, rather than just a brief day of frustration.

Did he grieve when somebody died in his care? Absolutely. It was always difficult to not approach it as a personal failure. Death was part of life, no matter how feared. Accepting that, even when he was ten years into his career and desensitized, was impossible.

However, Shadow had become less of a patient and more of a friend. Even if his friend never talked, he still cared deeply for the man. He wasn't someone to save. Cyril had worried time and time again about having a savior complex, but found himself rejecting the idea that Shadow needed to be saved at all.

Underneath all the trauma, Cyril saw the person Shadow would've been, had the trauma not clouded his sense of self. Shadow didn't need saving, not at all. He needed a mirror so that he could see that person through the fog. Cyril was determined to be that mirror.

Now that Shadow seemed to trust Cyril, Cyril didn't know how to best keep that trust. Shadow was still very fragile. No matter how much progress he was making, a few wrong actions or words could easily set him back.

Cyril didn't feel ready to be the object of such deep trust. However, he doubted there would ever be a day where he felt ready.

Eventually, Shadow's crying slowed. With the same gentle care that Cyril had shown him the entire time, he led Shadow over to the fireplace.

"I'll make you some hot chocolate. I have some of my cakes I made a few days ago."

Before he left Shadow, Cyril wrapped him in his weighted blanket and another blanket from Shadow's bed, just to be safe. Shadow was staring blankly at the fire. Cyril knew the empty sort of feeling that was left after such strong emotion.

He gave Shadow's shoulder a little squeeze before he left for the kitchen. Cyril wasn't hungry, but was worried because Shadow hadn't eaten yet that day.

Cyril remembered an old adage from his childhood – there's always room for sweets. He popped the leftover coffee cake in the microwave to warm it up for

Shadow. Then he worked the cocoa, sugar, and milk on the stove to make hot chocolate.

Once the two were ready and the coffee cake was the perfect not-too-hot, not-too-cold temperature, he brought them over to Shadow.

“Here. You need to eat.”

Shadow looked at him with empty hazel eyes.

“It’s okay to eat, Shadow. I promise.”

Shadow nodded a bit and took the cake and hot chocolate from Cyril. Quietly, he began to take little bites from the coffee cake and little sips from the mug of hot chocolate.

When the coffee cake was gone and the mug was empty, Cyril was absolutely relieved. He felt a little pride in himself, too. He could still think on his feet without his garden.

“It’s okay, Shadow, I promise. You’re safe here.”

Shadow nodded fully, then looked to the side. The cat had curled up next to him.

“Let’s wrap up your burn.”

Chapter 17

The next day, an air of an empty sort of uncertainty hung between the two of them. After the previous day's events, Cyril didn't know how to approach Shadow. He wanted Shadow to speak more, but he didn't want to push him too far.

Cyril concluded early in the day that Shadow was unlikely to talk to him without prompting. Prompting him to speak, though, seemed to be the problem. Shadow was still extremely fragile. If he made one wrong move or said one wrong thing, Shadow could go back to not talking at all, even with prompting.

Well, since he'd whispered his apology, Shadow hadn't said anything else. Cyril didn't know for sure that Shadow would say anything, did he?

There was only one way to find out.

Cyril wiped the sweat off of his forehead. Even if the days were getting colder, the sun was no less hot at noon. Well, at least, not until the clouds set in, but that was a little while away still.

When Cyril realized he should go make lunch, he gathered the courage to say something to Shadow, something that might get him to talk.

Shadow was sitting over by the fireplace with the cat purring in his lap. He looked relaxed for a brief moment before he saw Cyril in the doorway. It filled Cyril with a certain guilt, seeing Shadow go from relaxed to his normal anxious stoicism because he'd entered the room.

What was he planning to say again? Cyril couldn't remember.

Then it struck him. "I just realized." Cyril pretended to chuckle to himself. "We never gave the cat a name."

Shadow looked up at him and shook his head a little. Cyril hadn't the slightest clue as to what that was supposed to mean. That they hadn't? That the cat did have a name?

"Do you have something you're calling the cat?"

Shadow nodded.

"Can I ask what you're calling her?"

Shadow pointed to the orange-yellow patches on her coat. Cyril looked at Shadow, a little confused.

"You're calling her Orange?"

Shadow froze. That wasn't the answer and Cyril knew that Shadow wouldn't dare to contradict him.

Cyril walked over to Shadow. "It's okay to tell me in any way you can."

Shadow looked away in shame, then pointed towards the fire. The cat let out an unhappy noise when Shadow stopped petting her. Shadow clearly noticed because he was quick to start petting the small cat in his lap again.

"Fire? Flame? Ember?"

Shadow looked almost pained.

"Can you ... tell me with words?"

Shadow hesitated, then found his strength. His voice was no more than a whisper and raspy from disuse. "Whatever pleases you, Master."

Master. It was Cyril's turn to freeze. That was something he'd need to work on with Shadow. He worked to cool his temper a bit.

Nobody should've ever required you to say that, Shadow.

"It would make me happy to know what you're calling her."

Shadow looked down at the kitten, purposefully dodging Cyril's gaze. "Amber," he whispered.

"Amber?" Cyril repeated. "Like the color?"

Shadow nodded. Cyril glowed a bit with pride.

"She's Amber, then. It's a lovely name, Shadow. You did a good job picking it. I couldn't have come up with anything better myself. I was just calling her 'cat.'"

Shadow looked hesitant, like he was caught between two impossible options. What those options could be, Cyril didn't know.

Cyril didn't want to lose his chance to have Shadow talk more. He understood that every word was an incomprehensible effort, but he figured that the more Shadow talked, the less scary talking would be.

"Did you pick that name because of her fur or her eyes?"

Cyril didn't receive a response. Amber was purring a bit, but Shadow seemed to have left for a different world. He didn't know what to say or do further, so he figured that it would be best to leave Shadow with his thoughts.

With a small sigh, Cyril headed to the kitchen. After all, food fixes everything.

Shadow clearly needed to work at his own pace. It wasn't easy, overcoming that level of trauma. Cyril understood. He knew what it was like, in some vague way. Pushing Shadow would only make him retreat further into his shell. If Cyril had any hope of helping Shadow recover, he needed Shadow to be able to communicate in some way. Hell, he didn't even know Shadow's name.

He allowed himself to feel that frustration, but reminded himself that it wasn't about him. It was about Shadow.

At least he'd gotten five words out of him.

***

Sacha couldn't believe that he'd *chosen well.* He'd made a choice in naming Amber in the first place. He knew he shouldn't have. He couldn't name Amber in secret. It wasn't his place. He was a slave. He couldn't have anything of his own. It was selfish to have named Amber without first consulting what Cyril called her.

However, Sacha could tell that Cyril's praise was sincere. He was happy to hear Sacha talk. He liked the name that Sacha had *chosen.*

God, Sacha wanted to roll over and die. He was embarrassed to have revealed such a stupid name. He was a stupid slave, so all his names would be stupid.

Sacha looked down at little Amber, purring away quietly in his lap. His anxiety melted away. Would Cyril really use the name he picked for her?

In truth, it hadn't been because of her fur or her eyes. As Sacha pet her gently, he allowed memories of the great before to flood him.

As a child, he loved digging in the dirt, didn't he? Yes, his mother had always warned him to be careful of stray fishhooks down by the bay where he loved to dig the most. Besides digging, he also loved the driftwood that washed ashore.

He would never forget the day he found that beautiful orange rock while digging. Sacha had taken it home and shown it to his mother.

"Amber!" she'd proclaimed with a big smile. "You found amber, Sacha."

She helped him polish the stone into a shiny, only slightly opaque gem. Oh, how he showed it to everyone proudly, even if the other boys made fun of him.

When he was gifted his first sailboat – a smaller boat handmade by his father – Sacha named it after his childhood love: Amber.

In one way, he was entirely uncreative. He named everything dear to him Amber. In another, he was dedicated to his love of the gemstone and the happy memories it brought him. Not even Master had been able to taint his love of the gem – partially because he never knew.

What would Cyril think, if he knew the truth? Would he make fun of him like the boys from his village for loving a gemstone so much? Would he praise him?

Another anxious thought struck him. Maybe he'd upset Cyril by not speaking more. A silent funk had overcome Cyril. Maybe he was angry at Sacha for not answering his questions.

Even though he was scared of Cyril being angry, Sacha realized that he wasn't really scared of being hurt. Rather, he was scared of letting Cyril down. That disappointed, partially angry look Cyril had when Sacha burnt his hand the day before stuck with him. He never wanted to see that type of pain on Cyril's face again.

After all, Cyril had never punished him or made him work. Cyril had never hurt him. Cyril was kind and made him food every day. He made sure that Sacha had a bed. He even moved it when he wanted to be closer to the fireplace.

He owed Cyril. Sacha owed him a deep debt he was afraid he would never pay off. Cyril didn't want it in blood or flesh. So, how did Cyril want his repayment?

Why did Sacha trust Cyril not to hurt him? Master had been kind, too, in the beginning. He later explained that it was more fun to gain the trust of his slaves before he broke them completely. What told him that Cyril wasn't going to do that, too? What indicated that he could trust Cyril?

Sacha didn't know.

Sacha wasn't sure he wanted to know.

If he knew, he might be vulnerable enough to trust *another* person, beyond Cyril. That thought was unimaginable. Sacha would never trust anyone again, he'd promised himself. So, why did he trust Cyril? Why trust his current Master?

Sacha hated himself and reminded himself that he needed to work in order not to be hurt. If Cyril really was mad at him for not speaking more, he needed to speak more, even if that seemed impossible.

Cyril was nearly done cleaning up the kitchen from their lunch of leftover tomato soup, something Sacha could do easily with the burn on his hand. He'd gone through much worse. He could be useful and help Cyril and not be abandoned like a bad slave like him should have been.

Yet Cyril had told him gently once he'd gotten up from the table to go sit by the fireplace. Of course, he obeyed, even if it meant being useless.

The only way he knew how to be useful to Cyril was to talk, but what would he say?

It took everything in Sacha to muster up the courage to speak. He needed to say something. He needed to make Cyril happy. He needed to stay with the only person left he could trust.

With a raspy voice from years of disuse and electrocution, Sacha found the courage to say only a whisper to Cyril.

He walked over to the kitchen where Cyril was beginning to pick up his gardening tools in preparation for going back outside. Cyril was looking at him, with Amber curled up in his arms. Sacha couldn't meet his gaze, so, instead, he looked down at the cat.

"My name is Sacha."

Chapter 18

Sacha's first week of silence

The world was achromatic. In fact, for all Sacha cared, the sun might as well have been a myth. It wasn't like he would ever see the sun again. No, he was Master's and his role was to do exactly what Master said. Please him at the end of the day and hope that it would bring mercy the next day.

How long had he been gone from his family? Surely, they all believed he was dead. Simply put, Sacha well and truly had nothing. He didn't have his freedom. He didn't have his dignity. He didn't even have his voice. Everything was gone, forever.

The pain would never end, he realized. Even if Master was content to leave him alone that day, Sacha knew that tomorrow would bring only more suffering.

He couldn't continue on.

He was dirty. He was disgusting. He was a shell of his former self. He hated who he'd become.

He'd seen himself in the mirror of the bathroom the night before. He was thin with ribs poking through, covered in bruises and scars. Even if Sacha could go back to his family, it would be too humiliating. He never wanted to see them again, not with the marks of his failure along his body.

Master had been kind at one point, hadn't he? The first week, right? He'd shown Sacha mercy, only to rip it all away one night when Sacha was starting to trust him.

Sacha cringed at his own stupidity.

Since that first week, Master had shown him one simple mercy that was currently laid in his cell: a glass of water and a bottle of pills. Master had ordered him to not do anything stupid with it, but what did his orders matter if Sacha was dead?

He'd take control back. He wouldn't allow Master to own his life. He'd rather have no life at all.

Nobody was going to come for him. Nobody would cry when they saw his dead body. In fact, Sacha's body would probably be discarded in the forest somewhere, left to rot with the leaves. He didn't know what he did to deserve such a fate, but he knew he couldn't continue on living.

Sacha always thought suicide would be full of emotion. Yet he found himself feeling completely hollow inside.

He grabbed the bottle. How much would it take for him to overdose? Was it an opioid or was it acetaminophen?

Sacha didn't know and he wouldn't find out until he took them all, he assumed. With little sips of water, he began to down them all. First two pills at a time, then three, then four, until all thirty were in his stomach.

Sacha was filled with a tingling sensation as he realized what he'd done. The label on the bottle read "morphine sulfate." He was really going to die, wasn't he?

It was what he wanted, anyway.

Right?

***

Everything in Cyril's arms went clattering to the floor. He couldn't keep the shock off of his face.

My name is Sacha.

Shadow had actually spoken without prompting. On top of it, he'd said his name. *His name.* He had one. He actually had one.

The panic from Sacha was immediate. He stayed frozen in place with Amber in his arms. However, Cyril knew that Sacha's panic took many forms. Sometimes, he froze. Other times, he ran and hid. To Cyril, Sacha seemed to retreat back into his own head, hiding from a reality he couldn't bear.

As Cyril stepped over his gardening tools, Sacha flinched backwards with his whole body. He looked like a deer in the headlights. His breathing was shallow. His eyes were huge. His skin had gone pale.

Cyril's heart sank.

Cyril could see the apology on Sacha's lips.

He hated that Sacha was so afraid. He hated that someone had ever made him feel like opening up about something as simple as his name was something to be ashamed of. He wanted to take that pain away. He wanted to make it all better.

"It's okay. It's okay."

He didn't know whether he was speaking to himself or to Sacha.

"Shadow – Sacha. Your name is Sacha."

Cyril's eyes were brimming with tears. It was the most beautiful name he'd ever heard.

He couldn't help himself. He began to cry.

Cyril looked at Sacha standing there – *Sacha*. The name suited him well, somehow. He was littered with scars where bruises had once stood and was just starting to recover from the emaciation he'd suffered when brought to Cyril. He'd noticed some stretch marks on Sacha's upper arms and suspected that there were more. After all, Sacha was filling out those ribs and starting to look healthy again. Stretch marks were expected after malnutrition and starvation. They were another type of scar, sure, but another that marked his resilience.

Sacha was strong. Stronger than Cyril could ever be. His name seemed like a testament to his strength, somehow. Someone who'd been through something very difficult and had come out the other side stronger.

As he approached Sacha, he could only think of one thing to say.

"Can I have a hug, Sacha?"

Sacha looked startled. Still, he listened, with some indecipherable emotion on his face. He put Amber down, opened his arms, and Cyril pulled him into a tight hug.

"I'm so proud of you."

***

That day what seemed like years ago, Sacha thought he would never speak again. He'd promised himself. To talk was to trust and to trust was to open himself to being betrayed. Sacha had nobody. That was why he'd tried to end his life the day after he made himself that promise not to let anyone hear his secrets.

If to talk was to trust, then did he trust Cyril? Did he really trust him enough to speak?

It had been dumb luck that he'd survived the attempt, anyway. The doctor who just happened to walk in and just happened to have Narcan and saved him by reversing his overdose. Why? Why had that all happened? Why had he survived?

Was it for this? Was it for him to finally escape Master, like the doctor had always wanted?

Had some higher power willed him to survive just so he could escape and be here?

"Sacha, I understand that you can't talk a lot yet."

The gruff, tattooed man that stood before him – the retired doctor that lived alone in the forest – was crying. He was crying for Sacha. He was crying and couldn't keep his voice level like he had all the times before when Sacha had shown him trust.

Why was he so emotional? Why did Sacha's words matter so much? He wasn't supposed to speak at all.

"We're going to talk at your pace, okay? I'll wait. I'll wait until you're ready, okay?"

Sacha nodded a bit. It was impossible to think of a time where he could trust enough to talk like back then. Back before Master and slavery and having to please someone. Back when he had free will and happiness.

Would he ever have them again?

Something in him wanted to *ask* Cyril why he was so emotional. He was a slave. He did what Cyril wanted. If Cyril wanted him to talk, he would talk, right?

Somehow, that mantra felt so completely and utterly hollow for the first time that he could remember.

No, it wasn't that way, was it? Not anymore, at least. He'd screwed up so many times. He'd hurt himself without his Master's permission. He'd ruined a meal. He'd spoken without prompting. He'd overstepped and assumed what his Master wanted. None of those times had he been punished.

Not once.

Did that mean that Cyril was safe?

If there was one person in the world who was, Sacha realized, it was probably Cyril.

He never judged Sacha. He never got angry. Sometimes, he was frustrated, but he was never angry. He understood. He cared about Sacha in an unconditional way that Sacha couldn't comprehend – at least, not yet.

Sobs formed in his chest.

If Cyril was safe, Sacha was safe.

He wouldn't be hurt.

He wouldn't have to serve anyone.

He wouldn't need to be afraid.

That feeling of safety was foreign to him. After all, how could it be familiar? After the years with Master, he had no feeling of safety left. Yet here, with Cyril, Sacha could be safe.

Sacha hugged Cyril tighter, breaking down into heavy sobs. It was like a wound had been reopened in his heart. A wound in Sacha's heart that had never healed properly and needed to be reopened to be fixed.

His tears came pouring down in waves, like pulsating blood pouring out from that deep gash in his heart.

"D-don't leave," Sacha whispered.

"I won't, Sacha. I promise you."

Cyril didn't question the sudden tears. He didn't push Sacha. He simply moved with Sacha over to the couch and rocked him gently, carding his hand through Sacha's hair.

Ragged sobs escaped Sacha's chest. He was safe. He could hardly believe it. His body certainly didn't.

His heart believed it, though. His heart believed it fully and perhaps, that was enough.

Chapter 19

When was the wind not bitter?

It felt like a silly question to ask. Wind always signaled change and change was always bitter. Whether the winds were warm or they were cold, the changes were good or bad, they were bitter.

Sacha had a lot of time to think about that, forced outside during a snowstorm. He was restrained with his arms above his head, stretched and tugging on his shoulders with each shiver, tied to a wooden pole to keep him upright.

Master had given him the mercy of some basic clothing, but it was nothing against the windchill. Sacha had loved the snow before that day, perhaps because he'd always had the warmth of a fireplace to combat it. Now, he had nothing but a thin piece of fabric to protect him.

Cold, hard snow pelted his face. His nose had long since gone numb. His fingers and wrists were tingling in their restraints and burning against the bitter cold of the winds. How long was Master going to leave him outside for?

What had he done to deserve this? He hadn't talked. Sacha had merely accidentally kicked him. Of course, Master didn't know it was an accident, did he? Sacha couldn't tell him it was. Master always assumed the worst of him.

Where pleading tears had once laid was a thin layer of ice. The tears had flash-frozen to his face in the bitter cold of the winds. He refused to cry again. It would only make his cheeks hurt more.

His fingers were beginning to feel like icicles. What Sacha wouldn't give to be inside. Every breath was agonizing. The chilling air was freezing the walls of his lungs. Could he even cry with the wind turning the water in his eyes to ice?

Someone, please, help me.

The shivering, after all the time that Sacha had spent outside, was becoming painful. He was pretty sure that one of his shoulders had dislocated. Would it ever end? Maybe Master meant to kill him by leaving him outside. It seemed like an impossible mercy to die, even horribly and painfully outside.

Against the snow, Sacha saw the reflection of light. It was blinding, bouncing off of the ice all around it and burning into Sacha's eyes.

A warm, gloved hand grabbed his chin and made him look up. His cheeks, nose, and fingers felt warm and cold at the same time. Now, his chin was burning up under the heat of the gloved hand.

"Are you finally ready to behave?"

It was Master.

Sacha nodded frantically.

"I'm not sure that I believe you."

Sacha panicked and nodded. He would be good. He wouldn't kick again. He wouldn't even fight back.

As Master undid his fabric restraints and picked him up, Sacha was relieved and afraid. He leaned into Master's touch, happy not to be hurt.

He was changing. He hated it.

When was change not bitter, though?

***

The days had grown colder and shorter. Both Sacha and Cyril knew what that meant. Sacha just wasn't ready to face it. He'd long since learned that the cold was something to fear. Sacha couldn't say that it was something he hated – he had no opinions of value – but he found himself afraid of the inevitable snowfall.

Ever since the first time Cyril had taken him outside, Cyril had never insisted on it again. Sometimes, when the day looked warm from the clear skies and chirping birds, Sacha found himself longing to go outside. However, that was back before he *trusted* Cyril. Back then, he was still afraid that Cyril would think that he was attempting to escape.

Sacha had no desire to go out in the cold. Even if he felt that he could *ask* Cyril with *words* to go outside instead of just standing by the door, he didn't want to. The cold only brought back bad memories of things he wished he could forget.

So, when Sacha awoke to see Cyril making breakfast as usual with snow on his boots, Sacha's heart dropped. All he could do was sit and stare from his bed, wrapped in his weighted blanket.

Cyril was quick to notice his staring. "Is something wrong, Sacha?"

Sacha shook his head a little, but he'd already left the cabin. Suddenly, he was back outside in the bitter cold. The pain was overwhelming. He could feel Master's hands on him, trying to warm him back up. Sacha hated it. He hated the cold. He hated feeling so helpless.

Sacha came back to the cabin with the burning of cold ice in his hands. After that day, the feeling in his hands had never returned properly. As the ice cubes touched his hands and he saw Cyril's concerned face in front of him, Sacha screamed.

"Sacha, what's wrong?"

Tears formed in Sacha's eyes.

"Cold! It hurts, Master, *please.* Make it stop."

Sacha could hardly recognize his own voice after years of not using it. It sounded so weak and pathetic. Oh, how he hated himself and what he'd turned into.

Cyril immediately pulled the ice cube back. "I'm sorry, Sacha. I was just trying to help you with your flashback."

Sacha couldn't stand Cyril apologizing to him. He was Cyril's slave. He was safe with him and Cyril would not hurt him. But apologizing was still wrong.

After a long moment of silence and Sacha collecting himself from his panic, Cyril got the courage to speak again.

"Sacha, you know that's not normal, right?"

Sacha nodded.

"Did you ever see a doctor about that?"

Again, Sacha nodded. This time, he felt it right to speak. "My fingers are numb. They always hurt. They don't bend as much as they used to. Cold feels so much colder."

Cyril looked pensive as he looked Sacha in the eyes, trying to figure out what to say, Sacha presumed.

"I'm going to ask a difficult question. Did whoever kept you before you came to me ever leave you out in the cold? Is that because of frostbite?"

"Yes, Master."

Cyril looked shocked, but the look quickly disappeared from his face. *He must be getting used to it.*

"I'm so sorry, Sacha. Is there ... anything else that's wrong? Any other damage like that?"

Sacha was quiet for a long time. Of course, the answer was yes.

"I don't want to burden you, Master."

It was Cyril's turn to be quiet for a long time. "I'm a doctor, Sacha. You're supposed to burden me. I don't see it that way, anyway. I help people. I left medicine because I felt I couldn't. But I want to help you and if I can get you medicine to ease your pain, I want to."

The words came too late. Sacha sat quietly, thinking over the pain in his hands and toes. He didn't want to say any more. He'd already said too much.

Eventually, Cyril gave up with a sigh. "You can talk to me more when you're ready."

Sacha couldn't have been more relieved.

***

Cyril tried not to let himself be bothered by Sacha's latest revelation. He often wondered to himself why exactly it was so disturbing. By all means, Sacha had been through much worse and explained it to him, too. Was it the words that Sacha had used? The robotic way he'd said it? The way he called Cyril "Master"?

Cyril wasn't sure.

As he watched Sacha sit by the fireplace with Amber in his lap, he wondered to himself what other pains the man must've had.

Then it clicked.

It bothered Cyril because he could do something about it. He couldn't undo trauma. He couldn't fix neuropathy and frostbite damage. But he could make the pain more bearable, if only Sacha was willing to accept the treatment.

Then again, wasn't that what Cyril was doing in general? Wasn't he just making it so that Sacha could process his trauma in a safe environment without fear?

He couldn't do much, admittedly. He was only human. Nevertheless, the little that he could do seemed to be enough. Just like it took Sacha months to talk, it might take him months to accept that he didn't have to live in pain. It was his choice. It always was.

A moment later, Cyril realized he'd been staring when those hazel eyes moved up to meet his.

A question popped into Cyril's mind. "Sacha, were you upset by the cold? The snow?"

Sacha jumped a little. It seemed that he wasn't yet used to Cyril's nasty habit of staring at people while he was thinking of something to say.

"Yes, Master. It scares me."

Again, there was that word. Still, he'd admitted that something scared him. It was an impossible show of trust. Lord only knew what would've happened to Sacha had he admitted he was afraid of something. It would probably have been used against him to an unspeakable, unthinkable degree.

"Thank you for telling me." Cyril looked at him inquisitively. "Is that why you like it by the fireplace, Sacha?"

Sacha was quiet for a long time, thinking hard. Cyril was beginning to learn that it meant that Sacha was getting the courage to speak more than a few sentences. He was getting ready to say something big.

"It was cold in the basement, Master. I – I know that you don't have a basement here."

Cyril had a cellar that Sacha had never seen, but he didn't think it was right to interrupt Sacha to correct him on that.

"But I can't help but be afraid, Master. I – I didn't have clothes before you. It was cold every night. I never saw the light." Sacha's voice was starting to waver a bit. However, his eyes were distant as he stared into the fire. "If I stay here, I have heat and I have light."

So, fire represented something he didn't have before.

Cyril's heart sank despite the show of trust. Well, more accurately, his heart ached as he thought of Sacha alone, in a dark, cold basement, wearing nothing but a shock collar, waiting for whatever would happen next.

He thought of what to say, knowing that he needed to respond quickly. What was he supposed to say to that?

"I'm so sorry, Sacha. I know that doesn't fix anything, but I hope you know that I really wish that hadn't happened to you. Do you want me to buy you warmer clothes? Ones that would fit you better? Would that help?"

Sacha thought about the question for a while. Cyril was so worried to hear that Sacha was worried about being a burden again.

Instead, he heard a simple, "Yes, Master."

Cyril's heart sang with joy.

Chapter 20

Sacha had failed.

The beeping of the cardiac monitor attached to his chest told him as much. It had been a long time since he'd been attached to any such machinery. Did that mean that he was in a hospital? He sure hoped he wasn't. He hated hospitals. It was the last place that he wanted to be.

"You're awake."

An oxygen mask was placed over Sacha's face, but he had no need for words anymore. He turned his head to look at the doctor who Emery had brought to see him when Sacha wouldn't move a week or two ago. The doctor was the one who'd insisted on giving him pain medicine for his injuries. He'd given Sacha the means to an end.

"You're very lucky I had my Narcan on me."

Sacha begged to differ. He was anything but lucky.

Tears formed in his eyes. Soon enough, even though he was languid, Sacha broke down crying. The doctor, with all the gentleness in the world, took the oxygen mask off of his face to allow him space to cry.

Sacha could only pray that the doctor wouldn't tell Master that he'd intentionally overdosed.

Of course he would. He worked for Master, after all. Who would willingly work for Master, know about what he was doing, and not report everything directly to him? The doctor had to have something bad inside of him. Otherwise, why was he here?

The sympathetic look in the doctor's face did nothing to reassure Sacha. His rage was seeping into his eyes and once the doctor noticed, he looked away.

The doctor had taken away the one thing that Sacha had left – the chance at death. Sacha would never have another chance, not after failing. He couldn't help his anger, even if he knew he'd be beaten for it.

Sacha wasn't exactly angry at the doctor, though. His anger wasn't rational – Sacha knew that. If he wasn't angry at the doctor, then who was he angry at? Not at Master. That anger had faded away long ago and had since been replaced by despair and hopelessness. Not at the doctor. The doctor was probably just doing his job. Not even at himself. He'd taken a chance that he was sure would succeed. Was he mad at God for giving him the means to an end and allowing him to survive on dumb luck?

Yes, Sacha was mad at God. In the end, the morphine had been a cruel trick to make him hope for relief, only to have it all ripped away. Master was his earthly prison. He was *meant* to be a slave. It was what God wanted of him. If He'd wanted Sacha to be free, He would've allowed Sacha to die.

Sacha lifted the arm that didn't have tubing attached to wipe the angry tears from his eyes.

"I know you don't know me, Sacha, and I know that you're not allowed to talk to me, either."

Sacha could hardly focus in the depths of his despair. How could anyone be so cruel as to give him such an awful life?

"I – " The doctor paused. "Can you take some deep breaths with me, Sacha?"

Sacha did as he was told. That was his life now, anyway. The life he was destined to have.

Once he was calmer, the doctor spoke again. "I somehow convinced Emery not to punish you. By some miracle, he listened to me when I told him that wasn't what you needed. You skipped your medicines this month, right?"

Sacha nodded a bit, afraid that the doctor would give them to him.

"I know they're miserable, but you can't be taken off that quickly. I'll give them to you before you go."

Sacha's heart broke, but at least the doctor was being somewhat kind.

"I thought you should know, Sacha, that this is my last day here. I can't take it anymore."

At least you can leave.

"And I wanted to tell you that someday, I believe you'll leave. Just stay alive long enough for that, okay?"

Sacha nodded, but his promise was empty.

The doctor nodded back. "I'm truly sorry, Sacha. I – I hope that things get better for you."

They wouldn't. Sacha was sure of it.

However, the promise of no punishment held true, no matter how much Sacha didn't believe the doctor. Master left him alone for a few days, tended to his wounds, and didn't take Sacha back to his bedroom. Not for a week, at least. It was a mercy sent from a kind God, perhaps a different one.

For that, Sacha regretted having never thanked the doctor.

***

Sacha awoke that day with a runny nose. For a moment, Sacha might've believed that it was simply from the rotting leaves outside. He was allergic to mold. Autumn always gave him a runny nose.

However, when his vision went blurry, Sacha was quick to realize that the runny nose was an omen of something much more sinister. Soon enough, the lights were too bright, the noise of the water boiling on the stove was too loud, and the smell of the food in the oven was too intense.

It felt like he was being lobotomized. An icepick was being driven between the two halves of his brain, splitting them apart. The pain was unbearable. The nausea was overwhelming. He wanted to run away from the smell of the food and the light and the noise, the *noise* of the water boiling on the stove.

Sacha flinched as Cyril opened the door.

When did these attacks start?

Sacha shuddered at the memory. It was early in his captivity with Master. Master had turned the shock collar to its full strength and zapped him with all its power. Since then, he'd get migraine attacks. Master's physician had mentioned it was because of the electricity, right? That certainly hadn't stopped Master.

"Is something wrong, Sacha?"

Sacha shook his head. He couldn't be a burden on Cyril, not more than he already was. It didn't matter that the edges of his blurry vision were bringing him back to that awful cell. It didn't matter that he was in so much pain that he thought an icepick would launch out the back of his head.

The migraine didn't go away.

In fact, it stayed at that same, intense pain for days.

Sacha couldn't take it anymore. He resolved to *tell* Cyril. The pain really was going to kill him if he didn't.

Sacha knew that Cyril suspected something was wrong. He hated worrying Cyril. He wished that Cyril cared *less* about his health because he hated that he was causing Cyril any pain. But he just couldn't take the pain anymore. He needed to tell Cyril. Maybe Cyril could do something. Maybe telling him would make the pain go away.

"Master?"

"What is it, Sacha?"

Sacha hated speaking. He hated calling anyone Master, even if he knew it was the right thing to do.

"My head really, really hurts."

There were tears in Sacha's eyes. He felt so pathetic.

Cyril calmly approached him and mercifully turned the lights off. "Like a headache or a migraine?"

Through tears, Sacha whimpered, "A migraine."

Cyril nodded knowingly. "That's what was bothering you a few days ago, right? Has it been nonstop or is it coming and going?"

"Nonstop."

Sacha thought he would have a panic attack as he talked to Cyril. His throat was closing. Cyril was going to be angry.

"You should've told me sooner. I could've gotten you medicine so you don't have to feel like this."

Admonished. Sacha's crying quickly evolved into sobbing. It felt like such a silly thing to cry over. He'd been through so much worse. So, why was he crying over a migraine? Over Cyril offering to get him medication?

"I might still have some."

Cyril stood up from where he was kneeling in front of Sacha and went to what Sacha recognized as his medicine cabinet. He returned with a bottle and a needle in hand.

Sacha flinched back.

"Sacha, deep breaths. This is the best thing I can give you for the migraines. Come on, breathe with me."

Sacha followed along with Cyril as Cyril made him take deep breaths in and out, in and out, in and out. Eventually, his sobs slowed to cries and he could think somewhat clearly again.

"Migraines make people panic more sometimes. It's okay."

Cyril grabbed a pair of gloves and drew the fluid from the vial. It took everything in Sacha to not panic, to remind himself that Cyril wasn't drugging him like Master had. Gently, pressing on either side of the arm where he was injecting, Cyril pushed the liquid into Sacha.

"Come on, let's get you to bed. It should be better in a couple hours."

Cyril gently, perhaps with a little too much support, led Sacha over to his bed. Cyril pulled the sheets up on Sacha, making sure he had his weighted blanket to comfort him. Then Cyril went and drew the blinds on every window and turned off all of the lights.

"Try to sleep if you can, Sacha. I'll head out for a couple hours so everything's quiet."

Sacha couldn't have been more thankful, even if his arm really did hurt.

***

When Sacha woke up, he was sweaty as usual, but the light didn't hurt his eyes. The icepick wasn't going through his head anymore.

Tears found Sacha's eyes. He didn't have any of the pain or fatigue that haunted him after his migraine attacks. He felt normal. He actually felt normal. No more pain. No more tiredness. No feeling drained.

Cyril really had healed him. He'd actually helped Sacha with his headache. He'd taken the pain away. Sacha couldn't have been more thankful.

Cyril entered the room shortly after.

"Sacha, you're crying. Is everything okay?"

Sacha nodded. "My headache is gone."

Cyril smiled. "That's good. Why are you crying?"

"It – it – it's the first time that anybody has taken my pain away."

Cyril's smile faded. "I'm so sorry, Sacha."

"I'm in so much pain all the time, Master. My feet and hands hurt. I get these horrible waves of dizziness. I can never see properly. My hands always shake. There's always this horrible ringing in my ears, Master. It's never gone away since my previous Master. Then the headaches."

Cyril hesitated. His hand almost went to his nose bridge as it often did when Sacha did or said something that had to do with Master. Something had stopped Cyril – what, exactly?

The look in his eyes was complex and confusing, but Sacha could see the clouds of sadness somewhere in there. He'd almost expected pity, but didn't find any such emotion in Cyril.

Cyril didn't hesitate long. Sacha was sobbing. Cyril came over to Sacha's side and pulled him into a tender hug. He brushed Sacha's forehead gently, in a pensive way that Sacha wasn't used to.

"Thank you so much for telling me, Sacha." He heard the waver in Cyril's voice as he spoke. For a moment, Sacha thought that he'd upset Cyril. Cyril's voice so rarely wavered.

Sacha squeezed his eyes shut in an attempt to get his tears to stop. “I didn’t want to cry, Master. I feel like all I’ve done is cry to you, Master.”

“It’s *okay*, Sacha. You’re okay.” Cyril took a deep breath as he rocked Sacha gently, rubbing his back a bit. Cyril’s hugs were familiar to Sacha, familiar and comforting. It was exactly what he needed.

“I’m going to help you, Sacha. I’m mad I didn’t realize sooner, but I’ll do everything in my power as a doctor to help you, okay?”

New, fresh tears filled Sacha’s eyes.

“You don’t have to live in pain with me. I’ll fight to the ends of the earth so that you don’t have to, okay?”

Sacha nodded.

“Tomorrow, we’ll start. For now, you need to rest. You’ve had a long and, I imagine, a restless few days.”

Again, Sacha nodded, those tears of relief falling from his eyes and onto Cyril’s shirt.

He didn’t have to live in pain.

There was hope.

There was hope for *him*.

Chapter 21

Fear paralyzed every muscle in Sacha's body as the man behind him pushed him forward. Sacha's knees were still locked from having been locked in a human-sized cage for days, alone, with only one silent man coming to feed him twice a day. He felt stiff and old as he was pushed somewhere he didn't know.

"Move faster! We're on a time limit here, kid."

The men rarely spoke to Sacha, in fact. Sometimes, when he spoke to them, they would slap him in the face and tell him that he was just goods to be sold. Sacha didn't really understand what they meant until he was dragged into the cage he'd somehow learned to call home. The cage had made it all crystal clear. He was property. He was to be sold. He was a slave.

It struck Sacha only as the blinding lights of the shadowed room hit him that today was his auction day.

The grip on his hands that were tied behind him tightened. The crowd was maybe one hundred people, all wearing the most expensive-looking clothes that Sacha had ever seen. Sacha wasn't from a rich town. Quite the opposite, in fact. Seeing a room full of rich people was jarring.

They all looked so regal, so *normal*. It was a crowd that Sacha would've pictured at an opera, not at an auction of *people*.

"Here's our next pick of the night," the auctioneer announced to the crowd.

Sacha looked the auctioneer up and down, examining his clothes, his brown hair, his pale skin, all in hopes that he would someday be able to tell a police officer what his auctioneer had looked like.

"He isn't broken in yet. Despite his size, he's very strong and still has fight in him. Negative for all STIs and has no health problems to speak of. However, the highlight of it all is that he's from a small fishing village up north. His boat was wiped out in a storm and he's been presumed dead. No training to speak of."

The crowd let out some impressed, polite noises while Sacha froze. As his whole body went rigid, he heard the laugh of the man behind him.

How could his family think he was dead? Surely that wasn't true. How did they even know that a storm had wiped out his boat? Had someone else died and they assumed that because he was missing, Sacha was also dead?

Dread filled Sacha's stomach, making him nauseous.

If it was true, nobody was looking for him. He was doomed. He'd never be rescued.

"We'll start the bidding at $250,000."

Sacha didn't want to hear the numbers. He tried to shut his brain down to keep it from panicking. He didn't want to be there. However, that kill switch in his mind was gone. Each number streamed into his ear. Each person that wanted to buy him bidding against each other.

Sacha felt absolutely sick.

"$750,000!"

"One million!" came a much deeper, more sinister voice that ran chills down Sacha's spine.

One million dollars. For his life.

Sacha had to fight to stay conscious.

In fact, he found himself fading. The man behind him said something, but Sacha didn't catch it. Time was speeding up and slowing down.

"Two million!" by that horrible voice was the last thing that Sacha heard before he went tumbling to the ground.

***

Cyril didn't know how to bring up Sacha's habit without scaring him off. It made Cyril flinch every time that Sacha called him "master." He knew that Sacha was probably beaten into calling whoever held the most direct power over his life "master." After all, it was probably true that Cyril could do whatever he pleased with Sacha and never face the consequences of his actions.

Sacha's whole situation deeply bothered Cyril, but he knew one thing for certain: their relationship wasn't a slave-master one. If anything, Cyril considered Sacha a friend or some sort of adopted family member – the little brother he'd always wanted to have.

Cyril knew Sacha didn't see it that way. However, the longer he chose to ignore the "problem," the more normal it would be to Sacha. He needed Sacha, for his sake and Sacha's, to understand that Cyril wasn't his master. He didn't need to be afraid of him.

The question was how to say all that without scaring the poor boy off? Sacha would see it as a total rejection in all likelihood.

It wouldn't be easy, but it needed to be done.

Cyril waited until one of Sacha's "good days" to bring it up. Amber was curled up in Sacha's lap and Sacha was hand-feeding her some leftover fish.

"Sacha, I, um ... " Cyril immediately lost his nerve as Sacha looked at him with so much attention, looking so ... content.

Cyril took a deep breath. "You don't have to call me 'master.' That – that's not what we are. That's not what you are to me."

Sacha looked at him with utterly heartbreaking confusion.

"What ... what do you mean?"

The tears in Sacha's eyes startled Cyril.

"You aren't my slave, Sacha. You're a person. You're my friend. You aren't my slave. I don't own your life."

"I – I don't want to be someone else's slave."

Cyril froze. "I am *not* selling you."

He didn't expect his voice to come out in a growl that startled Sacha.

"I'm sorry. I'm sorry. I never meant to imply that. I never meant to imply that you weren't my owner."

Cyril took a deep breath. The whole situation was unnerving him more than the thoughts of having to have the conservation were.

"Sacha, listen to me."

Sacha perked up, a soldier coming to attention.

"You're not a slave. You're a human being. Human beings are not to be sold. That's just downright wrong." Cyril flexed his hand a little, steeling his nerves. "Just call me Cyril. Don't call me 'master.' I care a lot about you, Sacha. You aren't going anywhere. And I'm certainly not selling you away, okay? So just call me Cyril. Not master. Okay?"

He waited for confirmation from Sacha, but found none.

The silence was deafening. Cyril could hear his heartbeat in his ears. He didn't know whether or not to push Sacha. He didn't want to scare Sacha more than he already had, but he couldn't bear the silence any longer.

"You don't want to be called Master?"

Cyril shook his head, relieved. "No, just Cyril."

Sacha nodded.

They went silent again.

"He – " Sacha started, but quickly stopped.

Cyril's heart skipped a beat as he waited for Sacha to start talking again.

"He told me that if I was going to talk, I might as well be respectful to him."

"Respect is earned, Sacha. That man did nothing to earn your respect. He was awful to you. You didn't deserve any of it."

Sacha hesitated. Cyril could see from the look on his face that the concept was novel to him.

"You don't have to respect whoever kept you before, Sacha. We don't have to respect people who hurt us. If he ever hurt you because he felt disrespected, know that he more than earned that disrespect."

Sacha was quiet for a while. Again, Cyril didn't push.

Then Sacha spoke. "He did hurt me. When I wouldn't call him Master. Then for calling him Master. He liked me quiet."

Cyril's heart shattered, but not for the first time. In a solemn, but gentle, voice, he tried to repeat what he'd said.

"That isn't how people earn respect, Sacha. They earn your respect by doing things so that you trust them. They earn it by being kind. They don't earn it by beating and assaulting you. That isn't right. Okay? It's okay to not respect whoever kept you before. None of that was normal. That isn't how most people are. Respect is a two-way street and he certainly didn't show you any."

Sacha again looked perplexed. "A-are you sure? Not that I'm questioning your wisdom. I'm just – it'll be – you know, hard."

Cyril threw his hands up a bit in the air with a little shrug. "Of course it will be."

"I-I'm sorry! It was stupid of me to ask." Sacha huddled a bit in that way he always did when he panicked. He was protecting his stomach and face. Cyril wondered how often he'd been hit there.

"I didn't mean to be condescending, Sacha." Cyril, admittedly, was getting a little frustrated. However, he put aside his frustration. As he'd said multiple times before, it wasn't about him, it was about Sacha. "Sacha, it'll always be difficult. He did a lot of things to you. I'm sure you have a lot of complex emotions about what happened. It's okay to feel conflicted and unsure. It'll be hard to undo all that conditioning."

Cyril moved closer to Sacha. "Can I hug you?"

Sacha nodded. Cyril pulled him into a tight hug and rocked him a bit, even if Sacha wasn't crying.

"You've worked so hard already. You've come so far, Sacha. You talk. You help. You have someone you care about. The way you care for Amber warms my heart every day." He pulled Sacha a little closer. "Never forget how much progress you've made. None of it has been easy, but you've survived this far. You can survive and come back better on the other side of all this. I'm sure of it."

Sacha was quiet for a very, very long time. So long, in fact, that Cyril thought he would go quiet for the rest of the day. Well, perhaps not thought – worried.

However, Sacha defied that worry.

"You – do you really think so?"

"I don't say things that I don't believe."

Sacha let out a heavy breath, like he'd been holding in his breath for years and finally felt he could breathe.

"As long as we're alive, there's hope. You're alive and here with me, Sacha. You'll be okay."

Again, the two of them went quiet in their embrace. Amber was standing off to the side by the fireplace.

After a long time of that peaceful silence, Sacha whispered, "Thank you, Cyril."

Cyril smiled, his heart swelling with pride. "You're welcome, Sacha."

Chapter 22

Sacha knew that Cyril dreaded going to town. So, when Cyril announced that he wasn't just going into town, but that he was taking Sacha with him, Sacha was shocked.

Cyril must've seen the shock on his face, because he immediately explained himself.

"I made an appointment for you with an eye doctor. I ... um ... I have a phone that I have minutes on. Don't use it enough to justify an unlimited type deal. They were willing to take you in for today. If your vision is really as bad as you say it is, we can get you glasses."

Again, Sacha was shocked. *Glasses?* What had he done to earn glasses?

"I'm sorry, Master, Cyril. I just don't understand."

Cyril let out a small sigh. Sacha flinched.

"Your migraines. They can be made worse if you don't wear glasses and you need them. Your eye health is part of your whole health. I'm a doctor. It's my job to make sure everything is healthy. So, we're going to get your eyes checked. Okay?"

But I didn't earn it.

Of course, that little voice in his head that sounded an awful lot like Cyril began to tell him that he didn't need to *earn* glasses. Glasses were something people needed, not wanted. Needs were a given and wants were for earning, right?

Sacha didn't feel completely sure. He'd done well without glasses. Why would he *need* them? It wasn't like there was a life beyond slavery for him, anyway.

"Sacha?" Cyril could see that Sacha's mind was in a different place. Sometimes it was scary how well Cyril knew him.

Sacha nodded, showing he was back at attention.

"You deserve to be cared for. One day, you'll learn to care for yourself again." Cyril swallowed. "I won't abandon you. I swear. But I want you to be able to be independent again, one day. Glasses are part of that. You'll have a life again."

Sacha didn't believe him. There wasn't a life beyond slavery for him, not anymore. Maybe, if he'd found Cyril when he hadn't yet been ruined, there would have been hope for him. Sure, he was talking again. Sure, he was able to feel safe around Cyril. Sure, Cyril even said that they weren't slave and master.

None of it changed his nature – the nature that had been beaten into him by iron and willow.

"That's in the far future. But, for now, I just don't want any incidents like the spilled soup, okay? We'll get through this together."

Sacha breathed an inaudible sigh of relief. He couldn't imagine pretending to be a person again, not so soon. Cyril just wanted to prevent him from messing things up. Well, probably from hurting himself again, now that Sacha thought about it. He'd directly stepped on Cyril's authority – the authority he used to not hurt Sacha, to protect him and keep him safe. He'd endangered himself.

"Come on, let's get you showered."

***

The walk to the eye doctor's office was agonizing. The stares of the people's eyes unnerved Sacha as they looked beneath his warm, wintery clothes and onto the scars that laid beneath. Sacha couldn't help but feel like everyone was looking at him, silently judging him for what had happened.

Did they know that Emery kept him? Did they know who Emery was?

Every time someone spoke, Sacha found himself jumping a bit. How could he be expected to speak to the doctor? How would he face the doctor alone? It would be silly to make Cyril come with him just for an eye exam. He didn't want to be a burden.

I'll come with you if it would make you feel safer.

Sacha didn't know if Cyril meant it in a protective way or in a defensive way. However, he decidedly wouldn't burden Cyril with his problems anymore than he had to. He would go and see the eye doctor alone. He would do anything to pay Cyril back if he needed glasses.

A kind lady at the reception desk greeted them. Sacha didn't realize that Cyril had booked the visit very late in the afternoon until he saw the lights partially turned off and the empty waiting room.

"You must be Sacha Galanos?"

Sacha realized that Cyril didn't know his last name or his birthday. How had he booked an appointment for him?

"Yes, ma'am, I am."

The lady at the reception desk looked like she must've hated Sacha. Wasn't it normal to call a woman ma'am? Wasn't that just the polite thing to do? That was something from before Emery. Had he already messed it all up? Was he going to be punished when he got home?

Cyril put a hand on his shoulder, reassuringly, and squeezed a bit. The look in Cyril's eyes told Sacha that everything was going to be just fine.

"Alright, the doctor is ready to see you right away. You're our last appointment of the day, so I apologize for it being so dark."

"It's okay."

Cyril gave Sacha a small look, a question. It was the moment to decide.

Sacha shook his head.

Cyril nodded and moved towards the seats in the waiting room. The receptionist was the one who led him in the back. She left him in a quiet, somewhat dark room.

Next, another woman came in. She was dressed in plain scrubs and had her hair tied back.

"I need to put eye drops in. The first ones sting and numb your eyes. The next ones will make everything very bright. You'll need to wear glasses and wait a bit for them to kick in."

Sacha nodded. He could take pain. He could be good.

She helped him move to a chair where she leaned his head back and put the eye drops in. The first ones stung a lot, but the pain quickly faded beneath his watering eyes. As he blinked away the water in his eyes, he couldn't feel his eyelid moving over his eye in the strangest way. For a moment, he was scared. Would the feeling ever go away?

"First time?"

"Um, yes."

"It goes away in about an hour. I'm sorry. It really is a strange feeling, isn't it?"

Sacha nodded a bit. She smiled at him and hurried to put in the next round of eye drops.

"The doctor will be in soon," she told him as she handed him a pair of sunglasses made of plastic and paper.

The doctor came in shortly after and introduced himself. Together, they went over his medical history, why he came in, and what to expect out of the visit. Sacha had never been to doctors much throughout his life, but this felt like standard fare.

"Sacha, I just have one more question for you." The doctor paused. "I have to ask this to everyone. Are you safe at home? No one's hurting you, right?"

Sacha was a little taken aback. At first, he didn't really know what to think. However, the answer came to him easily.

With a small smile, Sacha responded. "Yes, I am safe at home."

"Okay, good. Let's get started, then."

***

The exam was over. His vision was still blurry and the lights felt particularly bright, but Cyril was smiling when Sacha showed up through the door.

"Sacha tells me you're a doctor, Cyril?"

Cyril nodded, looking at Sacha with the pride of a father watching his baby walk for the first time.

"Sacha has cataracts and is very near-sighted. His vision is 20/150. I highly recommend he get glasses."

Cyril looked at Sacha, then back up at the doctor with a small look of concern on his face. "Do you know somewhere we could get them done today?"

The doctor looked at Cyril and sighed. "I can have them ready for pickup tomorrow, same time, but it'll be extra. You can pick your frames now."

Cyril waved his hand, though Sacha was a little unnerved at the idea of Cyril having to pay more than he needed to for his glasses. Plus, pick his frames? Why did that matter? He was a slave. He should have the cheapest frames possible.

Cyril had a different idea.

"That's no problem. Thank you for being so accommodating."

The doctor waved his hand in return. "It's no problem."

Sacha could tell that the doctor was very annoyed with Cyril from the twitch in his eyebrow and the sarcasm in his voice. It made Sacha freeze up. Would the doctor hit Cyril? How would Sacha react if that happened?

"Thank you," was all that Cyril said, nodding a bit before taking Sacha to pick out his frames.

Immediately, Sacha was overwhelmed. There were so many options. However, Sacha's eyes were immediately drawn to one pair of frames. They had silver temples and rims that were a combination of thin silver on the bottom and dark brown on the top.

The price tag for them read $250. Compared to the other frames, they were certainly more expensive. Sacha instead went to the cheapest ones he could find and brought them over to Cyril.

"These ones."

Cyril looked conflicted for a moment.

"Are you sure, Sacha?"

Sacha nodded. *Don't question any further,* please.

Cyril went over to the ones that Sacha had wanted. He'd seen Sacha looking at them. Sacha's heart sank.

"I saw you looking at these and – " Cyril put them on Sacha's face. "I think you look a lot better in these. Come look at yourself in the mirror."

It was true. The other frames were thick and black, made of cheap plastic. These gave his face a nice shape. For once, Sacha looked in the mirror and not only saw himself completely, but thought that he looked *good*.

He recognized the man in front of him.

"They do look a lot better," Sacha conceded.

"Would you rather have these ones?"

Sacha hesitated, then eventually decided to take the risk. "Yes, I would."

Cyril nodded and smiled. He took the glasses off of Sacha's face and brought them over to the woman who was working the glasses. "We'll take these ones."

As the two left after Cyril finished putting in the order, Cyril smiled over to Sacha. They were alone on the side street that led to the eye doctor's office.

"I'm proud of you, Sacha. You did really well today."

Sacha glowed with pride. He'd done well. He'd made a decision and done well.

Was it really possible that Cyril had told the truth? That he didn't think of Sacha as a slave?

For once, Sacha allowed himself to hope that it was true.

Chapter 23

Sacha had never dislocated his jaw before. However, when Emery tied the bit gag around his face many sizes too small as a punishment for talking, Sacha suddenly understood the agony of having his jaw dislocated.

It felt like he would never be able to talk again. The pain was overwhelming. He couldn't even close his mouth or swallow his own saliva. Emery hadn't fed him in days. It didn't really matter, though. Sacha would've never been able to chew the food. Not after Emery placed the gag on his face.

Sometimes, Emery creeped in like the wind, only bringing attention to himself by rattling the bars of Sacha's cage. That was exactly how he appeared that day, a pair of hazel eyes coming to meet his and rattling the door on his cage.

"Oh, good, you're still alive in there." Emery smiled wryly at Sacha. "Remember my promise from when I bought you?"

Of course Sacha did. *I'll make your heart, body, and soul mine. You'll never leave me.*

"So you do." Emery looked immensely pleased and grinned his Cheshire grin. "Today, we make your body mine."

Sacha's eyes widened, which only earned a laugh from Emery. "Don't worry, Sacha. Today isn't the day that we'll have our first night together. No, that's a while down the line. You need to be better trained before we have our first night."

Emery's words sent Sacha into a panic. What, was Emery promising to rape him? To make him a sex slave? Sacha forced himself to hold back tears. His breathing was growing ragged. The world was spinning, but he soon realized that Emery had grabbed his hair and was dragging him across the room to the stairs.

He wanted to scream that he could walk, but Emery didn't care. Using a combination of his hair and his collar, Emery dragged Sacha step by agonizing step up the stairs.

When they emerged upstairs, Sacha felt the heat from the fireplace. He saw a red-hot poker in the flames and smelled the faint tinge of iron in the air.

Sacha shook his head and began to thrash. Emery was going to brand him. Emery was going to *brand* him! Sacha tried to scream, but all that came out was a garbled noise.

Emery dropped him on the floor and stomped on his already aching jaw. Sacha let out another garbled scream, a small keening as Emery rubbed his boot into Sacha's jaw.

"Don't you fucking dare make a sound."

Sacha whimpered a bit, which only made Emery lift his boot and stomp on Sacha's jaw. Sacha heard a horrifying *snap*, followed by the worst pain of his life.

His jaw was broken.

He was sure of it.

Tears rolled down Sacha's face, but the worst was yet to come. Emery secured his arms to the legs of the couch, forcing him down in a horrible uncomfortable position.

Then came the poker. The pain bit with white-hot, blazing fury as Emery touched the tip to Sacha's chest, carving "E.A." into his side in practiced, methodical cursive. Sacha couldn't take the pain. It was unbearable.

It took what felt like a few minutes for Sacha to register that he was crying and screaming. For a while, it sounded like the screaming was from a totally different body in a totally different space and time. Sacha only realized when his throat was so sore he started coughing.

Emery slapped him. "Still. Or I'll make this longer."

That was it. Sacha was never getting out, was he? He would always bear the mark of his Master. He would always be this man's slave.

If he had the power to brand and torture Sacha, Emery certainly could kill him in cold blood once he became bored.

The thought only made tears spill out of Sacha's eyes more.

He would never leave.

When Emery finished, he smiled. "See? Now you're mine forever."

***

Sacha dreaded going back into town again the next day. He was beginning to understand why Cyril hated going into town so much. The people stared and whispered. Sacha was always left to wonder if he or Cyril were what was attracting their attention.

However, Cyril brought him at an early morning hour when the only people on the streets were in a rush to go to work. For a moment, Sacha realized he'd forgotten how regular people lived their lives. They went to work and came home with their spouse and kids. They ate dinner as a family. They had friends and went out for drinks.

Sacha found himself feeling robbed. His life might've been idyllic to someone who was tired of the monotony of that life. Someone made food for him. He was expected to do little other than take care of the house and the cat. In many ways, he was still a slave, just a very pampered one. Maybe a treasured pet was the best way to look at it.

Was that a good life? Was that really what his life was? Sacha didn't know.

However, as he put on his glasses for the first time, it felt like he was seeing detail he never knew the world to have. Suddenly, everything was clear. There was so much more color. There was so much more detail. The leaves out the window in the distance had definition and shape.

Sacha couldn't help himself. He teared up a bit.

What was this beautiful world he'd missed out on his entire life? Was this really how people normally saw the world? It felt like he'd gone his entire life living in some ugly, fuzzy world and had suddenly joined the world of the living.

Cyril looked at him with a bit of alarm, but the woman who'd given him the glasses just chuckled.

"It can be overwhelming when you see so clearly for the first time."

Cyril looked over at Sacha. Sacha couldn't stop looking around.

Finally, Sacha found his words. "Thank you."

The woman smiled. "Of course. Enjoy your new glasses!"

Cyril nodded his thanks and motioned for Sacha to follow him. Sacha was still stunned.

Once he got outside, Sacha couldn't stop looking around. He could read the signs. He could see the people. He could look at the dogs walking with their humans. He could even see the cracks in the pavement as he was walking.

Sacha couldn't wipe the smile off of his face. Before Cyril, he would've felt the need to be thankful for the glasses. To show his gratitude in any way possible. But, with Cyril, Sacha knew that his happiness was the way to give thanks, so he smiled. He smiled like he would never be able to smile again.

He'd look over at Cyril occasionally, looking at his tattoos and his face that was just starting to have wrinkles. He'd never noticed the bags that hung under Cyril's eyes so much before. Cyril was smiling, too.

Eventually, Sacha decided to try reading newspapers at a stand in front of a bookstore.

When he did, his blood ran cold. His breathing constricted.

Right there, in colorful ink, was Master's face. There was big red and yellow text above it. His vision was so blurry from the past that threatened to take over his reality that he couldn't make out what it said.

Sacha was frozen, the eyes of his Master staring right back at him.

"Sacha. Sacha, what's wrong?"

***

The newspaper read at the top in flashy text, "EMERY ABBERTON, CEO OF BIOAVANTRIX, DIES OF MYSTERIOUS FLESH-EATING DISEASE." Under it, the subtitle read, "The young CEO was said to have caught it in Florida. Health officials are calling it a stroke of bad luck. What you need to know."

Emery Abberton?

The name of the man and the company was familiar, but left a sour taste in Cyril's mouth. He only knew Bioavantrix for one thing: dirty dealings with an extended-relief form of morphine. As an emergency room doctor, Cyril had never been approached by the company, but knew someone in pain management who had. From what Cyril understood, their marketing was as sketchy as their CEO's wealth.

Cyril knew the look of recognition on Sacha's face. He understood the fear in Sacha's eyes well. Was Emery the one?

Cyril couldn't answer that question in public. Sacha was frozen with fear, a deer in the headlights. Cyril knew that he needed to get Sacha out of there before he broke down crying.

"Come on, let's get to the car."

Cyril gently put a hand on Sacha's shoulder, which made Sacha jump, but Sacha started following him to the car.

It must be really bad.

Once Cyril had Sacha securely in the car, he took off. He needed to find somewhere private to talk to Sacha. Home was too far away and the situation was too urgent to just wait until they got there.

Luckily, the village was small with little in between. Cyril decided on a secluded parking lot of some park where nobody was. He turned off the engine and looked over at his panic-stricken, anxious friend.

***

"Sacha, did you know that man? Emery?"

Hearing someone else say his Master's name made Sacha sick. In fact, Sacha thought he was going to throw up.

"Master, Cyril, I'm going to vomit."

Cyril looked surprised but hurried to help Sacha get out of the car before he emptied his guts in a bush alongside the parking lot. It took everything in Sacha not to cry. He didn't want anybody to know. Sure, Cyril knew a lot, but he didn't understand the depth of the control. He didn't understand the depth of the pain.

Sacha wanted to forget about it all. He wanted to go into his brain and rip the memories to shreds. He wanted to die and have his secrets die with him. His breathing was more heaving than breaths as he tried to calm down while Cyril moved him into the car.

Once they were back inside the car, Cyril just sat there and rubbed Sacha's arm while he finally broke down crying.

He didn't want anyone to know.

He didn't want anyone to see.

He didn't want to live if people would know who it was and the depth of the pain.

"Sacha, you don't have to answer me. It's totally within your rights not to tell me. Just ... was that man the one who did it?"

If Sacha was going to have to admit to Cyril that it was, in fact, Emery, then he thought he might as well admit to the rest.

"He was Master." Sacha could hardly get words out between his sobbing. "He raped me and tortured me and branded me and drugged me. Every day was agony. I couldn't live like that. I hated life. I was kept in a cage. It was dark and cold and muggy. I never had medical care or any sort of love. I hated life. I wanted it all to end. My jaw still hurts. My hands still hurt. He'll always own me. Just like he said. He'll always own my heart, body, and soul."

Cyril looked at him with a bit of surprise. Sacha hardly realized what he'd said.

Cyril was quiet for a long time, though, eventually, he spoke. "I'm so sorry, Sacha."

But at that point, Sacha was too far gone. Cyril didn't ask more questions, but Sacha would never have answered them. Eventually, Cyril started the engine and drove the two of them home.

When they parked in the driveway, Cyril finally spoke. "You just rest, okay, Sacha?"

"Yes, Master."

As Cyril helped Sacha – who felt he could hardly move because all his bones had been broken by what he'd just admitted – into the house and beside the fireplace, the two of them were eerily silent.

It was better that way, maybe, because even as Sacha looked into the fire that used to give him reassurance, the image of Master on the cover of the newspaper danced in the fire instead.

Chapter 24

Sacha knew that he was stupid to hope for anything.

However, when he was left alone in that basement, with no one visiting him but the doctor, Sacha hoped for *something*. What was it, exactly, that he'd hoped for? An end to Master's brutality? That Master, after his suicide attempt, had finally realized how awful he'd been?

It was pure foolishness that couldn't even be called hope, lest it disgrace that idea that had gotten so many through dark times.

The doctor had even explained to him that Master was giving him a *break* – a different doctor than the one who'd saved him. So why, then, did Sacha find himself hoping that it would all be over when Master didn't come to see him for two weeks?

Of course Master crushed that hope. Why did Sacha hope for anything anymore?

"I see you're still as beautiful as the last time I saw you, Sacha."

Immediately, Sacha knew what Master wanted. Master opened the door to his cage and locked handcuffs onto his wrists, holding them firmly as he forced Sacha up the stairs to his bedroom. The bed was already prepared.

Sacha felt too numb at the sight of the restraints all ready for his body, the toys and the whip ready to torment him, to even muster up the courage to cry. Instead, he stayed silent, just as Master wanted, while Master laid him down on the bed.

Master smiled and began to pet Sacha's hair. "You're so nice and quiet this time. I can tell that I'm going to enjoy this."

He ground his hips a little into Sacha. Sacha felt his mind leave his body. He couldn't stay present as Master undressed him and began to lock his hands and feet, moving him into position. However, even though his mind was slipping away, Sacha knew there was truly no escape.

"At first I was very upset that you attempted suicide, but having your life really put in danger seems to have done good things for you. I might need to pull you off of your medicine as punishment more often."

Sacha looked at Master in horror. Master was stroking the inside of Sacha's thigh like he cared about Sacha's pleasure. Of course, it was just a sick illusion. He was just being possessive. Sacha didn't want to be forced into sex again. He didn't want to be raped.

"You're so much more fun like this. It's a good thing that you were so weak that you failed to die. You and I are going to have so much fun together."

Sacha could hardly believe his ears as Master lubed him up and entered him. The microtears from the last time were long since healed and, to Sacha's horror, it didn't hurt as much.

"You make such a good whore. It's too bad, for your sake, that you'll never get the chance to die again. I'm so happy you were a pussy and failed."

Master moaned loudly and began to speak again. However, under the intense thrusting and the horrible words being whispered into his ears in a constant stream, Sacha couldn't understand what was going on.

If only he could forget it all.

If only he could die.

***

Even though Sacha could never attempt suicide again, Sacha found himself realizing that he still believed that he would never escape Master. It simply felt impossible that he made it out alive.

As Sacha watched the flames dance in the fireplace, Sacha remembered the promise Master had made to him after their first night together after his attempt: *I'll be the one to kill you. You're never getting out of here alive.*

In the end, it was Sacha who'd survived Master. He'd actually survived. Master would never be able to kill him. Master was dead.

Even just the thought felt impossible. How could someone as powerful and wealthy as Master die of something as simple as an infection?

He'd gone to Florida with his mother. Had Master's mother also caught the illness? How did Master catch it in the first place? Did such awful things really live in the water?

It occurred to Sacha that Cyril probably knew the answer. It felt wrong to ask him something so awful. It felt wrong to rehash whatever trauma had made Cyril leave the medical field in the first place.

However, something in Sacha knew deep down that Cyril would be happy that he asked a question at all. Sacha was such a burden on Cyril. Cyril deserved so much more than to have a housemate that cried and screamed at three o'clock in the morning. Cyril deserved someone who could care about him in a way that Sacha felt he simply couldn't.

If asking the question would make Cyril happy, then Sacha would do it. He needed to earn his keep if he still wanted to be there after all was said and done.

"Master?"

Cyril looked back at Sacha with a certain sadness in his eyes. Sacha was taken aback. What had he done wrong?

"Yes, Sacha?"

"What's necrotizing fasciitis?"

Sacha was holding the paper in his hands – the one that Cyril had printed for him. It was an article without a picture of Master describing his death. He remembered that the other magazine had mentioned flesh-eating disease. Was that the technical term for it?

Cyril was quick to answer that question. "Well, it's a flesh-eating disease. There's a few bacteria that cause it. Seeing as he got it in Florida, it probably entered from an open wound. That's typically how you get it in the water."

Of course, Cyril didn't need to ask why Sacha was wondering. He couldn't hide that he, too, was reading the articles on Master's death.

Realization washed over Sacha's face. Master never took care of his nails. Sacha's nails were always brittle and sharp. Master had kicked him in the stomach and Sacha had dug into his leg with his nails. It had left a deep cut on his leg.

Sacha had killed Master.

The wound that got infected was from his nails. Sacha was the one who'd wounded Master. Sacha was the reason he was dead.

"I – Is it a painful death?"

Cyril looked hesitant. "It's a very painful death. The bacteria slowly kills the tissue until it rapidly enters the bloodstream, where it causes the person to go into shock. In some cases, it can take only a few hours, in others it can take days. Emery should've called an ambulance but I'm guessing that he didn't because, well, you were trapped in the basement there, weren't you?"

It almost sounded like an accusation. Cyril knew that Sacha was awful and was the reason for Master's death.

Tears formed in his eyes.

"I killed him."

"No, Sacha, you did not kill him."

"I-I scratched his leg. The bacteria entered through there. Master couldn't have had any other cuts. I would've seen them."

Of course, Cyril immediately understood the implication underlying Sacha's words. Sacha had seen Master naked countless times.

"Sacha, take a deep breath. You did not kill that man."

Sacha had gone from crying to sobbing. He'd killed Master. Master couldn't call an ambulance because he was there. Master had a family. He had a mother that loved him. All that, everything, left behind because Sacha had scratched him.

It was a guilt that Sacha couldn't handle. He'd killed a man. Even if that man was awful and had literally bought his life, Sacha couldn't help but think that Master didn't deserve to die for it.

Cyril kneeled down in front of Sacha, putting a gentle hand on his shoulder. Sacha flinched away, at which Cyril lifted his hand, leaving Sacha alone, huddled sobbing in a ball.

"Sacha, listen. Even if you had killed Emery, you would still be justified. You went through hell. You aren't responsible for his death. Any attachment you feel, it's a lie. It's survivor's guilt. It's those complex emotions you have to work through now, as a victim."

"I'm ruined! I'm ugly. He ruined me. I have nothing left. If he's dead, what am I worth now? I'm useless. I'm hideous. He put his mark on me. I don't even know how you can stand having someone who bears another man's mark around. I'm always going to be his property."

Cyril grabbed Sacha's shoulders and looked him in the eyes.

"I don't see you as property."

Those words shook Sacha's entire world. He didn't know how to react under Cyril's grip. He felt himself shrinking in shame for not realizing it sooner.

"You're a human being, Sacha. You aren't a piece of property. I understand that you feel like his because you bear his mark. I-I've thought a lot about it. Can you give me a moment?"

Sacha nodded and tried not to cry more when Cyril moved towards his room.

***

Cyril took a deep breath, steeling his nerves. He wasn't ready to have this particular conversation right then and there, but there wasn't a better time that he could think of. Maybe, just maybe, it would help Sacha calm down a bit to know that he didn't have to be Emery's forever.

Emery. That name would never be the same to him ever again. How could someone do something so awful? It was hard to hold back his anger. It was hard not to feel a deep, burning hatred for the man who'd left Sacha in such a horrible condition.

He grabbed the pictures he'd printed off his computer and brought him over to the fireplace.

"Sacha, I want you to understand something."

Sacha looked up at him with a mix of fear, reverence, and despair that made his heart want to collapse in on itself. Cyril didn't know how much more he could take if Sacha really did relapse. He was only human and he was very, very tired. As much as he cared about Sacha, he could only take so much failure.

"You *were* a victim of horrible things. Now, you're a *survivor*. You've been to hell and back. None of it – absolutely none of it – is your fault. Your brain is playing tricks on you. You feel like property. I understand that. You can be free from that. I've been researching ways to help you escape those feelings put into you by that human trafficking you went through."

Cyril handed Sacha the pictures. They were brands covered with tattoos. All sorts of brands – burns like Sacha's, tattoos, and scarification.

Sacha looked up at him in shock.

"When I went through my big trauma, tattoos were a way to reclaim myself." Cyril motioned to the pictures. "There are people who will tattoo over your brand, your scars, so that you can have your body back."

Sacha looked back down at the pictures, thumbing through them carefully. On each one was a different brand and a different cover-up.

"It's an idea. I will never force this on you. But I know of someone who's agreed to do tattoos for you for free. She'll cover your brands and any big scars that would help to heal your mind. All she asks for is pictures ahead of time."

Sacha looked down at the faces of the people, the smiles in the after pictures.

"They're beautiful."

Cyril nodded. "And I'm sure that at one point, they felt just like you. Because they survived very similar things to you. You don't have to feel this way forever. You can reclaim your body. You can reclaim your mind. He's gone, Sacha. He's gone forever. You're free. Now, you can reclaim what was taken from you."

Sacha's eyes were swimming with an emotion that Cyril couldn't quite pinpoint.

"Do you really think I can belong to myself again?"

Cyril didn't hesitate. "Absolutely."

Sacha went quiet for a very long time, looking at the pictures in his hands. "Can I think about it?"

"All the time you need."

Sacha nodded a little, biting his lower lip.

"Thank you."

Cyril smiled when he didn't hear a "Master" at the end of the sentence. "You're welcome, Sacha."

Chapter 25

Dear Senator Gasly,

I apologize for writing this in typeface. I'm afraid that if I wrote it by hand, my tears would stain the page.

My name is Clementine Matisse and I am the mother of Sacha Matisse. My son disappeared two months ago during a storm. He was out on the water with his friends. His friends all survived thanks to the lifeboats onboard. The lifeboat my son rode in was recovered, but his body was not.

Recovery efforts for my son ceased only a couple days past his disappearance. My family has found no peace. We do not know if our son is dead or alive. Without his body, we have not been able to bury him. Instead, every day, I am left to fear the worst: he is out there somewhere, sold and traded across the border like so many from our area.

I am from a small fishing village. I understand that we are a very small and somewhat insignificant part of your district, with the city being half of it. I understand that we are water people who don't matter much in the modern days.

However, I write to you with a simple plea: help me find my son.

I am only human. I can only take so much heartbreak. Since my son has disappeared, this community has never been the same. My son's friends don't laugh as much. His girlfriend cries herself to sleep every night. The whole village has been eerily silent since my son disappeared. He was the life of this village. Without him, laughter doesn't ring as loudly.

All I ask for is more crews. More dogs. More divers. We need to find his body. It cannot simply be left as an unexplained disappearance. I understand that my son isn't some nice-looking young woman tragically taken from her home, but he deserves your attention all the same.

Thank you for your time. I hope that you take my words into consideration.

Signed,

Clementine Matisse

***

Dear Representative Rochehart,

My name is Pierre. My last name isn't important. Sacha Matisse was my closest friend. It's been three months since his disappearance. Where are you?

My mother told me that this letter needed to be well-worded and polite. I don't think that people who sit idly by when people disappear deserve that level of respect.

Frankly, where the hell are you? The crews came for a week last month, searched the lake, declared that his body wasn't there, and left!

What are you doing?

My best friend is missing and all you can do is send a crew for one week and then leave? Without so much as even publishing a missing persons report on him?

What if his body is in the forest? What if he's been kidnapped? I know that after three months, there's little hope of finding him alive.

You should see Sacha's mother. She used to be the kindest woman. Happy, cheerful. Now she cries when she sees a son with his mother. Sacha's mother has been through enough. You know it took her fourteen tries to have Sacha? And that after Sacha she tried three more times, with no success?

Sacha was her life.

Now, I've had to celebrate the birth of my nephew without him. He didn't get to see me get accepted into university. I would never have even applied to university without him encouraging me after my gap year.

I had a bet with him. $50 for whoever became a father first.

I'll always win that bet now. Sacha is gone and you don't give a fuck.

Respectfully,

Pierre

***

Dear Senator Gasly,

My name is Antonio Matisse. I am Sacha Matisse's father.

We are deeply thankful for the crews that came with the dogs to search the forest for his body. However, we cannot accept the explanation that he ran away. Sacha had a whole life ahead of him. He had a family that loved him, a girlfriend that wanted to marry him, and a group of friends that would've died for him. None of us know where he went off to.

I humbly request that you register Sacha as a missing person. We understand that he is not vulnerable in the way that you ascribe it. However, Sacha had no reason to leave. Please, for the love of all things Holy and the oath you took to protect the citizens of your district, find my son.

With my deepest respect,

Antonio Matisse

***

Dear Representative Rochehart,

I am writing on behalf of Acadia LeBlanc, the girlfriend of Sacha Matisse.

My sister had been stricken with grief, but she wanted you to know that she is deeply thankful that Sacha's missing persons status has been sent up to the FBI. If there is any hope of finding him, we now know that the full force of the United States government is the way that we will.

We are forever indebted to you for your work in ensuring that Sacha is brought home in whatever way possible.

I hope that one day my baby sister can move on. Sacha was a good man. He treated my sister well. I could've seen them getting married. I hope that we find an end to

Sacha's story, whether that be him dead or alive, for all of our sakes. Thank you for understanding how much this means to our small community. Thank you for still caring about us water folk. Thank you for understanding our need for peace.

We all hope that Sacha isn't being passed around. It's been a problem in our communities, people disappearing and being sold around. We elected you to help take care of that problem.

I hope you're considering human trafficking in your investigation. All we want is peace. We don't want to continue on thinking that Sacha could be out there, somewhere, in the hands of some sick creep.

With deep gratitude and thanks,

Gabriel LeBlanc

Chapter 26

It didn't take Sacha long to make up his mind. In fact, his mind was made up right when he saw those other human trafficking survivors in the pictures. Even if he'd never met them, he felt an immediate kinship with them. He wasn't the only one with scars. He wasn't the only one with a brand. He wasn't the only one with a Master.

He wasn't alone.

Part of Sacha worried, though, that if he showed too much interest too quickly, he might seem impulsive.

Now you're a survivor.

The words echoed over and over again in Sacha's head. He was a survivor, wasn't he? Sometimes, his trauma felt so small and insignificant. Other times, it was huge and suffocating. When he looked at those pictures, he began to wonder how his trauma compared to theirs. Did it even matter? He was a survivor all the same. He'd come out the other side. He was alive, somehow.

The next day, Sacha awoke and, for the first time in years, couldn't remember having had a nightmare. When he came out of that groggy fog, it was like a storm had cleared in his head.

Sacha was strong. Master's death wasn't his fault. He was safe. Everything was going to be okay.

So why, then, did he feel a lingering sense of grief?

It's those complex emotions you have to work through now.

How was he supposed to even begin to process what he'd gone through? How was he supposed to be held together? How was he ever going to get a job? How was he ever going to talk to someone who didn't understand like Cyril did?

The questions bothered him. He had a life ahead of him now. Was he going to be too weak to take advantage of the opportunity that Master's death provided him? It wasn't like someone else would come to get him.

Sacha decided to wait until the next day to tell Cyril what he intended to do.

How exactly was he supposed to address Cyril?

I don't see you as property.

Cyril wasn't Sacha's Master, was he? Should he call him Cyril, like he did before? Somehow, that felt right. Despite the years of training, Sacha found himself able to call Cyril and only Cyril by his name.

"Cyril?"

Cyril turned to him from his place by the door with a big smile on his face. "What is it, Sacha?"

Sacha took a deep breath. It took more courage than he cared to admit to speak to Cyril. To ask him for something. To be selfish for a moment and to think of himself. It felt so wrong. It felt foreign to have wants. However, Cyril had offered and Sacha knew that it was appropriate to take him up on his offer. Cyril was sincere. He wouldn't punish Sacha for taking him up on his offer.

"I'd, um ... " Sacha paused. "I'd like to get tattoos to cover my brand."

Cyril looked a little surprised, and a small look of concern washed over his face. "You don't feel like you have to for me, right?"

Sacha shook his head. "This is for me. I want to be beautiful like them."

Cyril's face got emotional in a way that Sacha had only seen a few times. He smiled softly at Sacha, his eyes glowing with pride. "Of course. You're perfect the way you are, but if this will help you reclaim your mind and your body, you should do it."

Sacha sat in silence for a while, running his hand over Amber's head as she curled up next to him. "I don't know what it would feel like to belong to myself, but I want to find out."

"You will, Sacha." Cyril's voice began to crack a bit. "You will. I promise you that."

***

The next part of the process was perhaps one of the most difficult. Sacha hadn't taken his shirt off around Cyril since the very first couple days. However, the tattoo artist had requested photographs of what Sacha's scarring and branding looked like to know how well she could do on it, and Sacha had to oblige.

"Are you sure you want to do this today, Sacha?"

Cyril had his camera ready. Sacha was sweating, shaking, and cold with fear. The contents of his stomach had come up in his throat and formed an immobile ball.

Finally, Sacha managed to speak. "Better now than later."

Cyril nodded. "I understand. I'll turn around, and whenever you're ready, take your shirt off."

Quickly, Cyril turned around. Sacha took a deep breath. As he moved to take his shirt off, he could vaguely feel the chains around his wrists and ankles, the hands of his Master on his body. Sacha's breath grew shaky with each movement of the fabric over damaged skin. Would Cyril judge him? Of course not.

"I'm ready."

Cyril nodded and turned around. Sacha hated the way his breath caught when Cyril saw the full damage to Sacha's body.

"Which ones do you want covered? It'll make it easier if we just take pictures of the ones you want her to work on."

Sacha took a deep breath. He looked over the tattoos that Master had given him. There weren't many of them, but each one was a horrible, painful reminder of what he'd been through. Most were words meant to degrade him, little inside jokes that Master had about him.

"I, um." Sacha tried not to cry looking at himself. He hated having to look over the scars.

Maybe it'll be easier once I start to cover them.

"Th-the brand. And I'd like to start covering the scars on my shoulders."

Cyril nodded. "We'll only take pictures of those ones. You'll, um, probably want to have your other tattoos removed, right?"

"Or covered. Take pictures of those, too."

Cyril took a deep breath and began his work. Sacha felt like he did back then, being appraised by sellers at the auction. He hated the feeling. It was like worms crawling under his skin. Even if he trusted Cyril, even if he knew that Cyril wouldn't wrong him, Sacha was afraid. He was right back to being on the bed with Master and on the stage being auctioned to the highest bidder.

Time passed slowly and quickly at the same time. Before he knew it and after what felt like hours, Cyril finally chirped that he was done.

As Sacha put his shirt back on without Cyril looking, he found himself still stuck with those phantom touches.

"Cyril." Sacha felt selfish for even thinking about asking for something, much less actually trying to ask for it.

"Yes, Sacha?"

Sacha took a shaky breath, working up the courage to speak. "Please don't be mad at me."

Cyril's face creased with concern. "I won't be, Sacha. What is it?"

"I just need to be alone for a little," Sacha blurted. If he didn't say it all at once, he was afraid that he would never say it.

To Sacha's utter shock, Cyril smiled a bit. "It's understandable, Sacha. I'll go work in my garden for a while. I'm not upset. I'm happy you're standing up for yourself, okay?"

Sacha nodded, though he didn't understand. Why wasn't Cyril hurt?

As Cyril left, Sacha found himself feeling empty. Sacha moved to the fireplace, picking Amber up and placing her on his lap. Quietly, he pet her, holding her close to his body. Eventually, she climbed up onto his shoulder.

Sacha smiled a bit. The weight of Amber on his shoulder grounded him and brought him back. He wasn't with Master anymore. He was with Cyril.

So, then, why did he feel Master's hands on him, even after all was said and done?

***

Sacha and Cyril sat at the dinner table in silence, as they usually did. Since Sacha had the pictures taken, he'd felt like he was back in the fog. Back with Master. Back under his thumb.

Sacha hated it.

The silence broken only by the clattering of utensils didn't last long, though. Cyril took a breath like he was about to speak, but didn't start speaking until a couple minutes later.

"The tattoo artist – Halifa – she said she can get you in for your first appointment next week." Cyril took another breath. "She said you'll need laser treatments for the tattoos, but she's very excited to meet you and wants to start covering your brand and scars as soon as possible. She'll go over the details about the laser treatments with you next week."

Sacha nodded a bit. "Thank you, Cyril."

Cyril looked Sacha in the eyes. "Something's on your mind."

Sacha jumped a little, his face flushing. "Um, it's nothing."

"It's not nothing. Even if it's just your feelings, it's okay to talk about it. It's okay to not be okay right now. You've been through a lot."

Sacha thought about what Cyril said for a while. He didn't want to burden Cyril with his thoughts. He didn't want to upset Cyril. However, something in Sacha told him that if he didn't tell Cyril, Cyril would be hurt.

"I can't believe he's dead."

Cyril put down his utensils and looked at Sacha, attentive and alert.

"It's just ... he was so powerful. How can he be dead? How can he be dead from something as simple as an infection? He was strong. He was healthy. If he died from an infection, what does that mean about me?"

"Absolutely nothing, Sacha. You're not weak because the person who hurt you was killed by an infection. Flesh-eating bacteria are very deadly, especially the kind that he had. It was bad luck, not weakness."

Sacha bit his lip, tears welling in his eyes. "But I *am* weak. I can hardly feel happy that he's dead. I just feel relieved and sad." Tears began to flow down Sacha's face. "Why did I go through all that just for Master to die from some random infection?"

Cyril sat quietly in thought for a while, looking at Sacha carefully. "Would you have wanted him to be brought to justice?"

Before Sacha could think, he blurted more. His mind was a pot of boiling water spilling all over the stove. "My family is poor. Maybe I could've gotten some of his money so they could live happily without having to work or worry. My life is worthless now. My body is ruined. It'll never be the same. I'll always need people. At least if I could give you or them money, my life wouldn't have been wasted."

The two of them sat in silence for a long time. Sacha was frozen with fear from admitting the truth about his family – that he had one at all. He hated feeling like such a waste of space, a burden dependent on other people. Maybe, just maybe, if he'd gotten some of Master's money, he would've been worth something.

"Sacha, I ... " Cyril hesitated. "You don't need to be able-bodied and healed to be worth something. Your life will always have infinite value, regardless of what happened and what will happen." Cyril looked at his fingers, resisting the urge to pick at them. "Sacha, people need other people. You aren't a burden for needing someone else. You've, um, taught me how damaging it's been to live here alone."

Cyril wrung his hands together. "I'm thankful to have found you. I'm thankful to have your friendship. I'm thankful to have been a part of your journey to recovery. So, please, don't say such awful things about yourself." Cyril stood up and moved near Sacha. "Can I give you a hug?"

Sacha nodded, his chest heaving with sobs. Cyril wrapped him in his arms, pulling him tight.

"Everything will be okay. You'll relearn your value, one day."

CHAPTER 27

The tattoo shop was in a surprisingly open part of the city. To the left, there was a cafe serving locally roasted coffee and to the right, there was a small hair salon. Sacha felt infinitely reassured by the private rooms in the back and the open shop in the front. Though it was a foreign city that was about a three-hour drive from the cabin and Sacha had never really liked cities, Sacha felt reassured that he wasn't going to the type of place where somebody would tattoo against someone's will.

Like what Master did to me.

Yet Sacha still found himself nervous. He hadn't discussed what type of tattoos he'd wanted with Cyril, though Sacha had an idea in his head. It felt wrong to not tell Cyril what he was doing. In fact, Sacha almost felt like he needed Cyril's permission before going through the tattoo designs that he wanted.

However, Sacha was able to tell himself that the thought was totally irrational. Cyril wouldn't want Sacha to need his permission. This was about Sacha reclaiming his body. To do that, he only needed his own permission.

Absentmindedly, Sacha rubbed his hand over his brand. Soon, it would be covered, out of sight, out of mind. It was impossible. It couldn't really be happening.

Except it wasn't impossible. As Cyril smiled at him and opened the door of the shop, Sacha felt a rush of adrenaline. It was actually happening. He was going to get his body back.

For a moment, happy tears pricked in his eyes. However, they quickly went away when a happy woman with long black hair wearing a thick, warm sweater and leggings approached the two of them.

"Hi! My name is Halifa. You two must be Sacha and Cyril?"

Sacha forced a nervous smile and held out his hand for her to shake. She politely shook it. "Y-yes, I'm Sacha and – that's Cyril," Sacha stammered.

Halifa smiled kindly at Sacha. "Well, it's a pleasure to meet you. I've heard so much about you from Cyril!" She gave Sacha a gentle, reassuring look. "It's okay to be nervous. I know this is a big step forward in your life. You have every right to be nervous. I'm certainly not here to judge you."

Sacha nodded, relaxing a bit. The woman was nice. She reminded him of people back home with her smile and kind attitude. While the thought made him a bit sad, Sacha could look past that to the present. He was here for a reason. Halifa was a good person. She was going to hide his brand and cover his scars.

"I have us set up in the back in a private room. This first meeting will be a consultation, then tomorrow, we'll start with lining the tattoo. I'll tell you today how many sessions I think each of them will take. It might be best to book up a hotel since you two live so far away."

She motioned for Sacha to follow her to the back. Sacha looked back at Cyril and smiled. "I can do this."

Cyril was hesitant, but nodded. He took a seat at the front while Sacha followed Halifa into the private room.

She motioned for Sacha to sit down in a chair across from a desk that was covered with paper. On top were the printed pictures of his brands and scars. Towards the back, there was a padded chair and all of her tattoo equipment.

"So, I won't have you take your shirt off until the end of this session. I know for many human trafficking survivors, that's a sensitive action. I understand if you'd just like to lift to show me, that's also fine. I'm giving you advance warning so that you don't have to feel like it was sudden."

Sacha froze. He wasn't used to being given so much regard by strangers, much less so much understanding. How could anybody be so kind to him so immediately?

"You – have you done this with other ... people like me?"

Halifa nodded and smiled. "I'm part of an organization that does tattoos for free for human trafficking survivors. I've helped a lot of other people in your situation. Sadly, there's a lot of people with a similar experience to yours."

There's a lot of people with a similar experience to yours. At first the statement seemed impossibly sad. Yet it wasn't difficult to think that there were many other people sold at auction the day that Sacha was. It wasn't difficult to guess how many thousands of people were being trafficked around the world. Sacha was one of many. Somehow, that made him feel better and worse at the same time.

"So, what were your ideas?"

Sacha had to sit in silence for a moment, thinking about what to say. "I – they're probably stupid."

"As long as it's not a lion with roses, I won't think it's stupid."

Sacha nodded – he certainly didn't want a lion or roses. "I'd – I'm from a fishing village. Cyril doesn't know that. But I grew up helping with fishing and stuff."

Halifa smiled and nodded, encouraging Sacha to continue. "I bet you know how to sail really well!"

"Yeah, I do." Sacha chuckled lightly, before he caught himself and stopped. Finally, Sacha found the courage he needed to say everything at once. "I'd like an albatross on my back. I have a lot of whipping scars. They're ... they're the most painful to look at, out of all of them." Sacha swallowed a bit. "My mom had a saying: 'Hold fast and whistle for the wind.' I'd like that on there. Then, for my brand, I'd like a wrecked boat."

"But you aren't a wrecked ship, Sacha," Halifa immediately responded. "You're a ship that's in repair. I don't want to tattoo something that'll be so negative on you, okay? You've given me a lot to work with, so I'll get the designs ready for tomorrow."

Sacha nodded. He began to take off his shirt, assuming that Halifa would need to see what was underneath. She shifted a little, but then grabbed paper and a pencil. Sacha heard a little gasp when she saw his back but tried not to think much of it. That was the reason he was here – to be free of that.

Once she was done, Sacha left the room and went and saw Cyril. Cyril was smiling with the look of a proud older brother. For that, Sacha could feel proud. He'd done something well. He'd talked on his own and he'd expressed what he wanted.

Some part of him felt infinitely stronger because of it.

***

When Sacha saw the tattoo designs that would be placed over his brand and his back, the breath caught in his throat and tears formed in his eyes. They were beautiful.

Halifa was smiling proudly as Sacha held them in his hands, looking them over. The one that would be put on his back featured a large albatross over a small map design, holding a ribbon that said "Hold fast and whistle for the wind." He had a long scar that ran along his spine, and Halifa had designed the ribbon to cover it completely.

The one that would go over his brand was perhaps the more shocking of the two. Halifa had drawn a grand, three-mast ship with patches in its sail and irregular nails in its hull over a beautiful ocean, sailing towards a lighthouse. There were even birds flying overhead. It would be much bigger than his brand, but Sacha didn't care. It was beautiful.

Under the ship were the words "Rise again."

"One of the songs I listened to for inspiration was called 'The Mary Ellen Carter.' I thought that part of the song fit you well, Sacha."

Sacha smiled, happy tears sliding down his face.

"It's beautiful."

Halifa smiled even wider. "I'm glad that you like them. How about we start with the lines?"

Sacha nodded. Halifa started with the brand. It took everything Sacha had in him to not be dragged into a flashback of all the times he'd been tattooed against his will. The pain, the discomfort, the needles poking at his skin – he remembered it all too well.

This time was different.

He was reclaiming what was stolen from him. Emery would never put another tattoo on his body. This was his choice. He was defeating Emery's memory. For once, the pain wasn't damaging. It was something he'd chosen. In fact, it almost felt good. It was cleansing his mind. It was cleansing his soul. It was *his*. Not Emery's. Not Master's. His.

As Halifa worked gently and carefully, she checked in with him. Sacha didn't need it. As he sat there, he thought about Master. He thought about *Emery*. Would he ever really be free from him? Why did it still feel wrong to tattoo over the marks that Master gave him?

He got lost in thought quickly, and the time passed like lightning before his eyes. Before Sacha knew it, Halifa announced proudly, "We're done for today!"

She brought Sacha over to a mirror in the room and showed him her work. As he stared at his reflection, whipping scars and brand covered with intentional, powerful black lines, he suddenly recognized himself.

It was Sacha staring back at him in the mirror. It was a different Sacha than the one that he'd been before, but he was still *Sacha*.

Tears formed again in his eyes.

He was free.

Sacha was free.

As he stepped out to see Cyril, happy tears in his eyes, he didn't catch what Cyril said. Instead, Sacha raced up to him and hugged him tighter than he'd ever hugged anyone before, crying into his arms.

"I'm free," Sacha muttered between sobs.

If Cyril said something to that, Sacha didn't catch it.

CHAPTER 28

The basement was always freezing cold. However, the "freezing" part was so much worse during the winter. When the winds hit the side of the house and the frost penetrated the ground, the basement was so beyond freezing that Sacha sometimes thought he was going to die.

Sometimes, Master would leave Sacha down there, just to make him freeze. It wasn't like he ever had a blanket. In that inconceivable mind of his Master, it was a worthy punishment, a worthy reminder.

Sacha's stomach hurt. His lips had cracked and his mouth was dry.

He was nothing.

It was almost as though "Sacha" didn't exist anymore. He was a being that served another's pleasure. If Master gave him a different name, he would gladly accept it. What was he, if he didn't even care for his name anymore?

He was a slave. He was perfectly shaped to serve Master's needs.

And serve he would. Master opened the door of the basement and Sacha, with weakness in his limbs from the days of starvation, kneeled with his head bowed.

"That's a good little slave, hmm?" Master purred when he saw Sacha kneeling perfectly. Master ran a possessive hand over Sacha's collar, feeling the leather and the prongs where the shock module touched his skin. "I should leave you down here like this longer. You're so good when I do."

Sacha had to stop himself from looking up, from shaking his head, from whimpering, even. Instead, he reached his arms out, the sign that Master had taught him.

"What do you want?" Master cooed.

Sacha moved his arms up and down Master's pant leg, pulling a bit at his waistband. He would service Master. He was there for Master's use and Master's only. His body belonged to Master. His mind belonged to Master. His heart belonged to Master.

Master smirked. "So, you want to spend the night with me, hmm?" Master grabbed him by the chin, pulling a pair of handcuffs out of his back pocket. "You can nod, pet."

Sacha nodded obediently and offered his wrists out. Master quickly snapped the cuffs on his wrists.

"Come on, let's go."

Like he was commanded by a god, Sacha moved. Though, perhaps, there wasn't a god beyond Master. Master was God. Master was *his* God. He existed for no one else, after all. He had no one else to worship.

***

Sacha stood in front of the mirror with Halifa standing behind him, smiling proudly with her arms crossed. He could hardly believe his eyes.

For the first time since he became Master's, he didn't even really notice the brand on his skin. Instead, there was a ship. A ship that looked eerily like the one he'd manned all those years ago, out on the Lake – the one that had been destroyed by the storm that left him stranded.

Tears welled in Sacha's eyes. Even if his skin hurt a bit, a realization hit him: the pain had been worth it. He wasn't Master's anymore.

It was like a cord binding the two of them had been severed. When he looked in the mirror, Sacha didn't see Master's pet, Master's perfect slave. It was like every time before, Master had his grip on him, like he was hugging Sacha from behind. Sacha didn't see the phantasm anymore.

Sacha was entirely his own.

With that, Sacha took a deep breath. For once, he didn't cry. Master didn't deserve his tears anymore. Sacha owned himself. Not Master. Master didn't own him anymore.

"Are you happy with them?"

Sacha couldn't help the waver in his voice as he looked over the covered brand and scars. They weren't just covered, though. It was like they were gone forever. They were his now, not Master's marks.

"I love them."

Halifa patted Sacha on the back a little, startling him. She was quick to apologize, but Sacha stopped her by taking her hands in his.

"Thank you."

His voice was full of emotion in a way that even Sacha wasn't used to hearing. He hardly recognized his own voice.

"It's okay, Sacha. This is what I do. This is why I do it."

Halifa smiled and handed Sacha back his shirt. Sacha put it on and stepped outside, ready to face the world.

After all, he wasn't Master's anymore. Master wasn't his world anymore. The world around him was his to face.

***

When Sacha came out of the back room of the tattoo shop with a confident smile on his face, Cyril was shaken to his core in the best possible way. There was something definitely different about Sacha as he approached Cyril and threw his arms around him. Sacha wasn't crying. In fact, he seemed ... at peace.

"He's all done." Halifa smiled at the two of them. "He has the aftercare instructions. I hope to see you two again!"

Sacha smiled and nodded at her.

Cyril didn't really know how to react. It was like Sacha had walked out of that room as a totally different person. Not in a bad way, either. Sacha seemed more, well, Cyril could only describe it as how Sacha was supposed to be.

He thought that Sacha's new burst of confidence was something worth celebrating. Cyril had heard of a good Greek restaurant in the area. He wondered what kind of food Sacha liked, if he would've tried Greek food before.

"Sacha, we're going out to celebrate."

Sacha froze a bit.

He doesn't want to be a burden on me, even for this.

"It – it's okay. We can just go home to eat."

Cyril looked Sacha in the eyes, leaning down a little. "Sacha, I *want* to take you out to celebrate. This is what normal people do. They go out to celebrate big accomplishments like what happened today."

Sacha again hesitated, but that newfound confidence seemed to take the wheel back a little bit. "Okay."

Cyril smiled and took out his phone. Since they'd been traveling back and forth to the tattoo shop, Cyril had taken out an unlimited everything plan with his network provider. He hadn't realized that just scrolling the news and watching some videos could take up so much data when spread over a week.

He pulled up walking directions to the restaurant and led them through the bustling sidewalks of the city to a small, hole-in-the-wall type place.

"It's Greek. Nothing too spicy."

Sacha blushed a little and chuckled self-deprecatingly. Cyril was shocked that Sacha didn't take it as criticism.

It made Cyril happy.

Together, they went in and Cyril ordered them a table. When the waiter handed them menus and left, Cyril almost expected Sacha to ask his permission to order something. However, Sacha surprised him yet again.

"Can I order what I want?"

"Of course."

Sacha nodded a little. "Then I'll have bakaliaros."

Cyril smiled widely, glowing with pride. It was like watching his younger brother walk for the first time.

That was what Sacha was to him, wasn't it? Sacha was his little brother – his little brother that needed protection and guidance.

Cyril smiled to himself.

He'd always wanted a little brother. Now, he finally had one.

***

On their way home, Cyril led Sacha to a tech shop. Sacha looked completely and utterly confused.

He looked even more confused when Cyril took him to the counter and made a specific request: an unlocked Android. The clerk was a college-aged guy with glasses who was eager to help them. He was quick to rush to the back with the price point and request that Cyril had given him.

Finally, Cyril turned to Sacha while the clerk was gone to get him their options.

"Sacha, you need a phone."

Sacha shook his head, seemingly overwhelmed. "No, I don't. It's too much. Three hundred dollars? Who would I call?"

Cyril gave Sacha a serious look. "It's independence, Sacha. If you need to call someone, if you want to access information about the world and to learn, you need a phone."

The clerk came back and cut off any semblance of a conversation that the two were having. He ran the two of them through their options, but most of the information was lost on Sacha. Cyril was quick to make the decision, though. He knew most of the models already from his own phone shopping and knew which was the best deal. All he needed to do was order the SIM card online.

When they left the shop, bag in hand, Sacha stopped the two of them.

"Thank you. Everyone keeps doing all these nice things for me. I don't really understand why."

Sacha's voice was filled with a mix of gratitude and sorrow that warmed and hurt Cyril's heart.

"You deserve good things. That's why, Sacha."

Sacha nodded hesitantly with a sincerity that Cyril wasn't used to.

***

That night, after Cyril helped him set up the phone, Sacha decided to search the one thing he promised himself to never search when he received the phone.

Into the search bar, he typed one simple name: "Emery Abberton."

Immediately, articles about his horrific death surfaced. Sacha didn't want to dig through them, lest he find something about his captivity being found out.

Instead, he scrolled over to the images and enlarged the first one he saw.

He stared at Master's face for a while. He was smiling pleasantly, well-groomed, very different from the man Sacha had known. It was hard to believe that Master and Emery were really the same person. It was hard to believe that he was gone at all. What had it all been for, if Master died?

Cyril was snoring a bit in his room by the time that Sacha came back to the present.

Sacha found himself wanting to talk to Master, or, at least, the picture of him on his phone screen.

"I outlived you. I survived."

Sacha's eyes brimmed with tears, blurring the image on the screen.

"I'm alive and you're not. I'm not yours anymore."

With courage that Sacha didn't know he had, he whispered at his phone, "My – my name is – it's Sacha Matisse, and I'm not yours anymore."

With that, he cleared his search history and turned off his phone.

He would never have to see Master again. Sacha would never be his again.

CHAPTER 29

One of the questions Cyril would have never been able to answer clearly was simple. What would happen if somebody he loved walked into the emergency department, dying?

Of course, there was always another doctor on call for that very reason. Nobody could act objectively.

Well.

That was the ideal. Sometimes, it happened, in those smaller, less-equipped hospitals, the more rural ones that Cyril found himself working at, that doctors were alone to manage an entire emergency department. Sometimes, the other attending called out sick. Sometimes, the residents just quit. Hours were longer in rural hospitals. The patients were sicker, poorer, more in need.

In cities, perhaps doctors were praised. In rural medicine, Cyril was lucky to see a patient before they cut their own melanoma off. A backache in the rural emergency department was never just a backache.

The night that haunted Cyril every night was a particularly bloody one, but not because of a gang turf war or nightclub mass shooting like in the cities.

No, the plague of the country was far less dramatic: oxycodone.

Well, oxycodone was how it all started, at least. It was like a hydra. Once the doctor who'd been paid to overprescribe left, the problem sprouted two more heads. Cyril remembered in high school when only a few people knew the word "oxycodone." Now, everyone knew it, along with heroin, codeine, and fentanyl.

All it took was one miscalculation and Cyril would be working twenty-four hours on his feet, fighting to save life after life that just didn't get Narcan in time.

They had a word for it.

Oxycuted.

Cyril never thought it would be someone he knew.

However, that night, when a bad batch had found its way into town, everything changed.

The attending was down with the flu. They only had one resident on staff. Cyril's eyes were red from a lack of sleep and far too many caffeine pills.

He wanted to go outside to smoke. However, there were far too many people pouring in, mothers with sons and sons with sisters.

Everything in Cyril's world fell apart when the stretcher with paramedics came rushing in the back.

"Code Blue. Code Blue."

Cyril froze. He recognized the face.

Oliver.

Oliver. The one he'd grown up with. The one he'd had his first cig with. The one that had asked him to start a band when he knew what little talent he had.

Oliver. His best friend.

What little food Cyril had managed to fit in between patients immediately came up. One of the nurses rushed over to him as he huddled over one of the hallway trash cans.

"Dr. Galanos, are you okay?"

Cyril shook his head. "It's Oliver. Oliver Marchmont."

The nurse looked at him sadly. "Dr. Galanos, you're the only doctor here tonight. I'll call Dr. Tharby to see if he can come in."

Cyril knew what that meant. He stood up, accepting the paper-thin tissue that the nurse gave him.

As Cyril had to test Oliver's reflexes to ensure his death after thirty minutes of trying to save him, the moment of peace they held for him didn't feel real.

However, when Cyril had to see Oliver's mother, tell her that her baby boy was dead, he couldn't take it anymore. Holding her in his arms as she cried and cried and cried was too much for Cyril.

That night, he cried as he smoked his last cigarette. Cyril never cried. But that night, he nearly jumped off a bridge from the depths of his sorrow. He felt like an awful person. Why was he the one who had to tell that woman, the one who was practically a second mother to him?

He would never return to the hospital.

In fact, after a few months, he never returned to medicine at all.

The farther he was from the hospital, the better. So, he moved where there wasn't one for thirty miles.

His little cabin in the woods.

***

Sacha awoke during the night in pain. It wasn't out of the ordinary, exactly. Sacha had lived most of his life since Master bought him in pain. Even then, five months after Master's death, Sacha was still in pain.

Cyril had explained that it was likely permanent. Nerve damage, he'd called it. Pain from injuries that never healed correctly, too. Those years of medical neglect and endless tortures had taken their toll on Sacha's body: neuropathy, migraines, essential tremor, tinnitus, vasovagal syncope, and a lot of other diagnoses that he didn't care to remember.

Luckily, Cyril wasn't Master. He gave Sacha medical care. He gave Sacha medicine. A pill of acetaminophen and a pill of ibuprofen did the trick most of the time. Cyril had offered to try to get him on longer-term treatment, but Sacha didn't like taking daily pills. He'd take medicine when he needed it.

That night, the pain was bad enough that he decided on two acetaminophen and one ibuprofen.

He rummaged through the bottles in the medicine cabinet and pulled out what he thought were the bottles he needed.

As he laid his head down, Sacha felt especially sleepy. The pain was going away in a different way than usual. Sacha almost recognized it, but the medicine was also taking away any worry that he might have.

Before long, Sacha's head hit the pillow and his eyes closed.

***

Cyril awoke with a start. Nightmares of the time before his cabin in the woods, that time before Sacha, had plagued him recently.

He was getting awfully tired of seeing dead bodies in his sleep. He was tired of seeing their lifeless eyes and their bleeding bodies. In some ways, his experience with Sacha had triggered it all to come back. He'd stopped practicing medicine because he didn't feel like he was actually saving people. Now, in order to save someone who genuinely needed it, he had to practice again.

Did Cyril mind? Not really, though taking care of Sacha was definitely taking a small toll on him. Well, maybe small wasn't the word. The toll wasn't insignificant, but it wasn't big enough that Cyril would want to get rid of Sacha. The very thought was repulsive. Cyril loved Sacha like a little brother. It was his job to take care of Sacha.

Eventually, Cyril decided to get up and get something to drink in the kitchen. He wasn't worried about waking Sacha up. Sacha slept like a log.

However, as Cyril brought a glass down from the top shelf of a cabinet, he noticed a bottle on the counter.

Hydromorphone, 5 mg tablets.

Why did he still have those damn pills?

Immediately, he turned to Sacha. Had Sacha taken them? Sacha often woke up in the middle of the night to take pain medicine. Cyril had tried to convince Sacha to switch onto something long-term, but Sacha refused. He never gave a reason as to why, but Cyril suspected that he had a fear of long-term treatment after being drugged for so many years.

Sacha was sound asleep.

Almost dead asleep.

Cyril took the pills out, counted them. Sacha had taken two. *He took two!*

Panic overwhelmed Cyril as he ran over to Sacha and shook him.

"Sacha! Sacha! Wake up."

At first, Sacha didn't wake up. Dread filled Cyril's blood like a poison. Sacha was dead. Sacha was dead.

He'd lost another one.

He couldn't.

Surely, he had Narcan somewhere. Maybe it wasn't too late to give it to Sacha.

"Sacha, wake up!"

Desperation filled Cyril's voice.

In fact, he didn't even realize when Sacha groaned. He was too busy looking through the cabinets for Narcan. He needed Narcan. He needed to save Sacha. He couldn't lose another person. Not another friend.

"Cyril, what's wrong?"

Cyril's breath caught in his throat. Sacha was standing, breathing.

"You – "

Cyril stopped himself from asking Sacha if he was dead.

The panic suddenly came crashing down, and Cyril felt tears in his eyes. Sacha wasn't dead.

"You took two hydromorphone pills."

"Two ... what?"

Sacha squinted at Cyril. He sounded pretty tired, groggy, but he was still there. A lot more calm than usual, but not anywhere near being dead.

"Opioids. I thought you overdosed."

Sacha shook his head. "I've overdosed before. I'm ... definitely ... tired, but not overdosing."

Hearing that Sacha had overdosed before certainly didn't calm Cyril down. However, he knew that he risked freaking Sacha out with his panic, so he quickly went to his room and slammed the door shut.

Cyril heard Sacha roll back over to bed. He'd ask in the morning what Sacha meant by that.

Still, he grabbed his shirt, placing his hand over his racing heart. Sobs broke through his chest. He kept himself quiet. He couldn't stand to have Sacha hear him cry.

However, Cyril couldn't hold it back anymore. He cried tears, remembering the dead body of Oliver laying on the bed. The cold of his dead skin. The hollowness of his dead eyes. Sure, the soul was impossible to prove from a medical standpoint, but from a physical one, a presence always left the room or was simply not there.

Oh, how Cyril longed to be in his garden, far away from the worries and fears that plagued him.

But it was winter. It was cold outside. There was no garden to tend to. Only the fears that he had to face head-on.

Chapter 30

When Cyril heard the other kids at his school talk about their families and what they were doing for Thanksgiving, Cyril couldn't help but feel a sense of envy. He knew it was a sin to hate others for something he didn't have. Cyril just couldn't help himself.

The people who ran the group home were good people, but they weren't parents. After all, they switched all the time. Just when Cyril thought he liked one of them, they changed. Sometimes, he got switched home-to-home. Moved around like a pawn on a chess board, but with a lot less care and thought.

Throughout it all, Oliver was there.

Oliver, the loud. Oliver, the mischievous. Oliver, his friend.

They were opposites but somehow both managed to be on Ritalin. Well, Oliver was on Ritalin. Cyril was on Concerta. But it was the same chemical for the same diagnosis, so they found a comradery. When Oliver got himself in trouble, Cyril was always there to save his ass.

Cyril was always afraid to lose him, but he never did. There was security in Oliver. When Cyril got moved, by some odd chance, Oliver always moved with him. In a way, they were a bonded pair of cats. They were unwanted strays, but they had each other.

Certain times of year were more difficult than others. November and December were always horrible months for Cyril. Holidays about family and love – both were things that Cyril didn't have.

Thanksgiving dinner at the group homes was always the worst. Donated turkeys and sides, pie baked by a charity. It made Cyril feel less human, almost.

So, when Oliver snuck a note under the table, telling him to go out "to the bathroom," Cyril took the invite to leave.

The two of them left out a window and went to the creek by their group home – their designated meeting spot in the rural jungle they found themselves in.

Oliver was smiling wickedly. That was never a good sign.

From his pocket, he pulled out a pack of Malboros.

"I got these at the store."

Cyril looked at them in shock. Oliver was grinning proudly.

"Did you steal them or something?" Cyril asked incredulously.

"Maybe," Oliver responded, pursing his lips jokingly.

"Oliver, that's a crime! What if they find out? You might get sent away."

Of course, being sent away was always the fear. Group homes were some sort of sick privilege – there was always worse. Cyril wouldn't survive without Oliver.

Oliver gave Cyril a small shove. "Don't worry so much." He pulled one of the cigarettes out of the box and offered it to Cyril. "This will help you relax."

Cyril took the cigarette from Oliver reluctantly. Oliver gave him a light the minute he had it in his mouth.

It was true. The cigarettes did relax him. Within ten minutes, he felt better.

Cyril sighed. "I'm just tired of feeling like this object of pity, Noll."

It was easier to talk without the weight of the fear of being judged hanging over him.

"I know what you mean." Oliver took a puff of the cigarette. "I had to sit through a talk about 'people who don't have families for Thanksgiving' and being sensitive and shit. I don't want their sympathy. I want a fucking family."

Cyril nodded a little. They were a bonded pair of cats, but they weren't really family. Just deep friends of the soul, perhaps.

"We're seventeen. It's over for us." Cyril looked down at the cigarette. "The fuck does my life matter?"

"Because you're here, Cyril. You're here with me. You're brilliant. You could become a doctor. Then nobody could tell you that your life doesn't matter. You have so much more of a future than me."

It was true – Cyril had a 4.0. Oliver had maybe a 2.9 on a good day. In a world where high school grades determined their futures, Cyril was someone who would thrive. Cyril loved his friend. He tried to convince him to try community college, but Oliver wouldn't budge.

Oliver was wicked smart. He had a good personality. All he needed was to believe in himself more.

After a while of silence, Cyril began to hum. It was "Born in the USA" – Bruce Springsteen. He always liked the opening. So did Oliver.

In fact, Oliver started singing, "Born down in a dead man's town."

Cyril began to sing along with him. "And the first kick I took was when I hit the ground."

Eventually, the two of them sang it with irony. "You end up like a dog that's been beat too much. 'Til you spend half your life just to cover up."

Yes, they were dogs that were beaten too much. It would take half a lifetime to cover it up. Cyril just didn't realize that yet.

They talked for a while longer until they came back stinking of cigarette smoke. They got yelled at, but it didn't really matter. Cyril was just glad to be with his friend.

***

Sacha awoke the next morning, thinking about the odd dream he'd had. Something about Cyril freaking out about needing Narcan. It had to be a dream – some odd mix of his past overdose and his housemate being a doctor.

His head pounded and he felt jittery.

What had he done last night? He used to sleepwalk. Could he have sleepwalked and hit his head?

When he went over to the counter, Sacha saw the bottle on the counter.

Hydromorphone.

Cyril's words came back to him. That was the medicine that Cyril was shouting about in the dream.

It wasn't a dream, Sacha soon realized. He really had accidentally taken two of a very strong opioid instead of acetaminophen.

Shit.

He'd told Cyril about his overdose, hadn't he? He didn't want Cyril to know. He didn't want Cyril to think him stupid or ungrateful or any other number of horrible things.

What would Cyril think? Surely after everything, he wouldn't abandon Sacha. But what if he was extra watchful? What if he forced Sacha on medication to ensure it didn't happen again, just like Master had?

Sacha forced himself to take a few deep breaths.

"It's okay. Cyril is safe."

That was right. Cyril *was* safe.

***

Something was wrong with Cyril. He hadn't spoken to Sacha much at all that day. In fact, he'd even picked Amber up in his arms and petted her gently. Cyril never picked up the cat. It wasn't that he didn't like her – Cyril was just always nervous about hurting her.

Was it because Sacha had admitted to attempting suicide?

Sacha didn't know, but he needed to say something, clearly.

"Cyril, I, um ... " Sacha took a deep breath. "I'm sorry."

Cyril was a little startled. "For what?"

Sacha started to quiver. "For telling you about my overdose."

An emotion resembling discomfort and remembrance flashed over Cyril's face, before he came back to his normal, concerned look. "It's okay, Sacha, to be open with me."

"It was different. I can tell something's wrong."

Silence hung between them for a while. Eventually, Cyril put Amber down on the ground, where she quickly walked over to Sacha.

"It's, um, a personal topic that I don't talk much about, my history with overdoses."

Sacha wasn't happy with that answer. In fact, he felt a little dejected. "Mine was a suicide attempt. It was the only time I ever had access to the means. It – it was dumb luck that I survived it at all."

It took all the courage that Sacha had to say the last part of what he wanted to say. "I've said mine. Can you tell me yours?"

Cyril sat pensively for a long time. Sacha's heart was beating out of his chest.

"I've never told anyone."

"Me neither." Sacha was desperate. He felt so useless. "You're always helping me and listening to me. Let me return the favor, Cyril. Please."

Again, silence hung in the air between them.

"It's a long story."

"I don't have much else to do."

Cyril chuckled a bit. "You've become so much more confident. Those tattoos really did change you."

Sacha cringed. Those thoughts came back. He was too confident. He was arguing. He was being disobedient. It was bad. He was going to be punished.

What should he say to prevent that? What could he do? Sacha had already argued himself into a corner.

"Calm down, Sacha. Take a few deep breaths, okay?"

Cyril's voice brought him back down to reality.

Right, he wasn't a slave anymore. He was safe. He was okay.

***

Cyril took a deep breath, wringing his hands together. He'd told his story occasionally when he needed to for essays and the like, but it was never a comfortable subject.

"I don't have a family, Sacha. I was a foster kid. I lived in a group home."

Sacha was listening so intently it almost broke Cyril's heart.

"I was transferred a fair bit, but there was this friend I had who was always transferred with me." Oliver's grinning face appeared in Cyril's head. "He was kind and happy and sweet, if not a bit scatterbrained and stubborn. He was the one who encouraged me to become a doctor. He was talented with writing. He helped me with my essays for college applications and again with personal statements when I applied to med school."

Those late nights they spent together came back to Cyril pleasantly. "He was my only connection to other people. But he struggled in ways I never knew. I presume he had what you'd call an addictive personality."

Cyril took another deep breath, his voice shaking. "I stayed where I grew up, as did he. He became an electrician – trade school. I worked at the only emergency room in the area. One day, there was a bad batch of heroin in the area. He turned up dead at the emergency room. My name is on his death certificate. I had to call the time of his death. I had to tell his mother – his mother came to be a part of his life when he was twenty. She was the one who convinced him to go to trade school. He was twenty-eight when he died."

Tears formed in Cyril's eyes. When Oliver had died, a piece of him had died with him. That hole in his heart hurt each and every time he thought of his deceased friend – the other half of their bonded pair.

"I never knew he struggled with heroin addiction. God, if I knew, I would've walked to the ends of the earth to help him."

Sacha moved quietly, putting Amber down, and moving over to Cyril. He pulled Cyril into an embrace.

For the first time, someone embraced him first – to comfort him.

Cyril broke down crying in Sacha's arms.

"That's hard. I'm so sorry you went through that. It – it sounds awful. Even with everything I've been through, I can't imagine having to call the death of your closest friend."

Cyril sobbed tears that he hadn't cried since he looked over the edge of the bridge that fateful day.

With Oliver's death, Cyril thought he'd lost all ability to form human connections. After all, he'd felt more like a stray cat or a beaten dog than a human being for most of his life.

However, as Sacha held him in his arms, he began to realize that it wasn't gone forever. No, in fact, he had another way to connect to people. It was Sacha. Sacha, the stray cat that Cyril had found on the verge of death. Sacha, his little brother that he needed to protect.

"I thought I'd lost the ability to have another human connection. It was so hard back then."

Cyril pushed Sacha back, tears still flowing from his eyes. "But I've found you. You're like a little brother to me. So don't give up on life. Okay?"

Sacha bit his lip anxiously and nodded a bit.

"I love you, Sacha. I really do."

To his surprise, Cyril heard back a response he never expected.

"I love you, too, Cyril. You're my family."

Chapter 31

The thought occurred to Cyril while he was lying in bed that night that Sacha probably had a family that was looking for him.

After that, thoughts raced through his head and he couldn't sleep. Though Cyril never had a family, he knew how important it was to people who did have one. It was the reason that not having one was such a loss.

Could Cyril just ask Sacha? The idea of asking Sacha directly didn't sit well with Cyril. Sacha had reacted so badly to finding out that his captor had died. How would he react to being asked about his family and having all that uncertainty about if they still wanted him? Sacha already believed that his family wouldn't want him. What if that was actually true?

Cyril needed to protect Sacha from that, if it was true. He didn't want his little brother to have to go through such severe rejection when he was so vulnerable.

Though it was Sacha's right to know what he was doing.

Cyril's thoughts were a mess. He got up from his bed and went to his desk, taking out a pen and paper. Soon, he started writing things down.

Sacha's family lives near a large body of water. They're sailors. They're also poor.

Those were ambiguous clues at best. A lot of water folk were poor. Oswego, Rochester, Buffalo, Syracuse, and Watertown. None of them were particularly wealthy. It probably wasn't any of the big cities, though.

Maybe Sacha wasn't from New York at all. He could be from Ohio, Michigan, Minnesota – maybe even Ontario or Quebec. With a name like "Sacha," Cyril could believe that he was from Quebec.

Did Sacha even know where they were?

As Cyril sat in his frustration, trying to figure out a starting point, an idea popped into his head.

Sacha went missing. There was probably a missing persons report about him.

Cyril opened his laptop. The time read 1:06 a.m. However, Cyril was wide awake. His mind was buzzing.

He quickly typed in "missing persons database" into the search bar. Soon enough, the National Missing and Unidentified Persons System flickered onto his screen. Cyril went to the tab for missing persons and began to type.

First Name: Sacha

Sex: Male

Race / Ethnicity: White / Caucasian

Height: 5' 8"

Hair Color: Brown

Eye Color: Hazel

By some miracle, there was only one result.

Matisse; Sacha; 19 Years; Hope, Chautauqua, NY; Male; White / Caucasian; 11/17/14

Cyril's blood ran cold as he clicked the line and looked upon a picture of his Shadow, Sacha. He read through all the details, read the report.

Sacha had gone missing in a storm. His mother was looking for him. So was his father. His grandmother was deceased. What if Sacha had missed his chance to say goodbye? The thought didn't sit well with Cyril.

Where is Chautauqua?

Cyril opened Google Maps. Opposite side of New York, near the Pennsylvania border. He was up near Alexandria Bay, up by the Canadian border. It was a five-hour drive. Not bad, all things considered, but still very far.

On the report, there was a phone number. His mother's – the house line and cell phone number.

Should he call? Just to see if they were active?

Cyril decided to. If it rang, he would hang up. He dialed the number of the house line into his cell phone and hit "call." The phone rang. Startled, Cyril quickly hung up and put his phone down.

Sacha had family and he could call them.

Cyril had to tell Sacha in the morning. Sacha needed to know. He needed to talk to his family. He needed Sacha's family to know that their son was still alive.

Anxiety filled Cyril. What if Sacha wanted to leave to go to his family? Of course, Cyril would let him, but it would be another loss of one of his only connections to other people. Cyril would survive, yes, but he'd never be the same.

Those were thoughts for another time. He needed to sleep. His clock read 3:34 a.m.

***

Sacha could always tell when Cyril had something on his mind. Cyril was unusually tired, like he hadn't slept enough. He kept telling Sacha that he was fine, he'd just had a bit of trouble sleeping, but Sacha was smarter than that. He knew that Cyril had something he was hiding.

However, Sacha didn't have to be the one to bring it up. When Cyril came back inside from clearing the path to the cabin, he had words on his lips.

"Sacha, I, um," he started. Sacha's blood went cold. Was he kicking Sacha out now that he was doing better? Had he screwed up?

"I found your family."

For a moment, Sacha's heart dropped to his feet and he thought he was going to faint. Cyril came over to him and helped him to the sofa.

"W-what?" Sacha asked weakly. He was seeing stars. He could hardly think. His family wouldn't want him, right? He was in such horrible condition. Nobody would want him. Nobody but Cyril, apparently.

"Take a few deep breaths, Sacha. Tell me some things that you can see."

Cyril guided him through the grounding exercise with the same care he always did.

"You – you're not looking to get rid of me, right?"

Sacha had tears in his eyes. He didn't know what to think. Did Cyril honestly find his family? Cyril was no liar. If he said it, it had to be true.

"Sacha, please look at me." There was untold emotion in Cyril's eyes as Sacha looked at him. "Sacha, I would never do that. Frankly, I'm scared of *you* leaving *me*." Cyril chuckled a bit to himself. "After we talked about what happened with me, you know, how I don't have a family, I thought that you probably had one."

Cyril took a breath, holding Sacha gently by the shoulders. "Your family filed a missing persons report for you four years ago. You've been missing four years. You're only twenty-three." Cyril chuckled a bit wryly. "Twenty-three and already been through so much. You're so incredibly strong, Sacha."

Tears formed in Sacha's eyes. He didn't know what to think. He didn't know what to say.

"The phone number on the missing persons sheet still works. I don't know if it's still the same landline, but we could try."

A rush of adrenaline filled Sacha and he stood up suddenly.

"Let me talk to her."

Cyril nodded a few times. "Yes. Yes, of course. Do you have your phone?"

Sacha had forgotten that he even had one. He pulled it out of his pocket and dialed the number that Cyril had pulled up on the digital file of *his* missing persons report.

Have they been looking for me this entire time?

Sacha could hardly believe it. He was in tears before the number was completely punched in.

The phone rang a few times before a very familiar voice picked up the phone.

"This is Clementine Matisse speaking. Who am I speaking with?"

"Maman ... "

The line went quiet. More sharply, the voice came back. "Who am I speaking with?"

"Maman, it's me. It's Sacha. I'm safe. I'm alive. I'm okay." It all came out at once. What was he supposed to say? After four years, he was finally speaking to his mother.

He started sobbing. "I'm safe, Maman. I'm safe. There's so many things I want to tell you. Just, I'm safe. Okay? I'm safe."

The line went quiet. So long that Sacha was afraid that his mother had hung up on him. She probably thought he was dead.

However, the sobbing on the other end of the line soon told him that he was very much on the line.

"Tell me," she asked between hiccuping sobs, "who did you have a crush on in first grade?"

Sacha laughed, flushing a bit. "Did you really have to ask?"

"Tell me who you had a crush on."

"Olivia."

The line went quiet. He heard someone whispering. "It's really him."

Both of them were quiet for a while. Then Sacha's mother was the one to speak. "Can we come get you?"

Sacha looked at Cyril, who was nervously watching him. Sacha smiled a bit at Cyril. "I'm up near Alex Bay, Maman. I'm safe, but I'm far away."

"Honey, I would travel across the world to come get you. Five, six hours is nothing."

It's your choice to make. It sounded like something that Cyril would say, coming out of that Cyril-sounding voice in his head.

"Just tell me where. I'll come get you."

"I'm with someone who rescued me. I'm staying in his cabin. Let me ask him where it is exactly."

Sacha turned to Cyril. "She wants to see me. What's the address here?"

Cyril froze a bit, but relaxed immediately in his normal, nonchalant way. He gave Sacha his address, which Sacha quickly repeated to his mother.

"We're getting on the road now. We're coming to get you, sweetie. You'll be home tonight. I-I'll call you when we're in Syracuse."

Then the line dropped.

Sacha looked at Cyril. Cyril was smiling with tears in his eyes.

"She loves you, Sacha."

"You heard?"

"You have your speaker volume very loud."

Sacha didn't realize that he never turned it down in the first place.

"I – "

"It's okay to not know what to think right now, Sacha. It's okay."

Sacha nodded and bit his lip. Then he ran to Cyril and gave him a big hug, sobbing.

He was going home. He was actually going home.

Oh, how happy he'd be when he was finally in his mother's arms.

Chapter 32

Sacha sat anxiously on his handmade bed, watching his phone. The phone call wasn't even an hour ago and it would take his mom and dad at least two hours to reach Syracuse.

He could hardly believe it. For all those years, he'd believed that he would never see his family again. He believed that they wouldn't want him. He believed that he was ruined. Now, they were driving to come get him. They still loved him after all those years. Hearing his mother's voice had made that clear. He wasn't ruined, not to her.

Cyril had a sad smile on his face. Sacha knew what he was worried about – he was worrying about it, too. Neither of them wanted to leave the other. They were perhaps a pair of bonded cats – one who'd been beaten and left for dead and the other who'd lost their bonded.

"Sacha, I – I wanted to say that I'm really happy for you."

Cyril's voice was full of an emotion that Sacha couldn't quite pinpoint. There was an air of sadness between them, even if it should've been a happy time.

Would Sacha's mom accept Cyril – the tall, gruff, tattooed ex-doctor with enormous difficulty accepting people into his big, broken heart? Sacha didn't know. She might find him bizarre. After all, Cyril was much older than him.

Sacha wondered – would she accept *his* tattoos? His scars? What if she balked when she saw him? He didn't look like her son anymore.

"Cyril, I'm, um, thankful for everything you've done."

Cyril nodded. "If I can't come with you, promise that you'll call me once in a while?"

Sacha sat there, stunned. Silence hung between the two of them. "You – you want to come with me?"

Again, Cyril nodded, this time more shyly. "I'm sorry. It probably seems strange. I'd – I want to move to Hope or somewhere close. I could open a practice. I've always done rural medicine. Maybe I could help you or your mother with aches and pains."

Tears formed in Sacha's eyes. "You want to practice again?"

Cyril took a deep breath. "You've shown me something I'd forgotten, Sacha. The majority of people in this world are good. They're resilient. They stand up against great evil. The bad aren't worth saving, but most aren't bad. After all, this whole world would be so fucked up it wouldn't function if everyone was bad. So, I want to practice again. Especially near your home."

"But – what about your cabin? Your garden?"

"I'll sell it. You mean more to me than a pile of sticks." Cyril looked around a bit. "It's ... probably better that I leave anyway. I'm at a different place in my life now. This represents a different time now. I can plant a garden wherever there's dirt."

The two of them sat in silence for a while. Though Cyril most often took care of Sacha, Sacha couldn't help but feel proud of Cyril. Cyril had softened a lot since he first met him. Whether or not that was because they'd grown inseparably close, Sacha didn't know.

"I think it does for both of us," Sacha eventually said.

Cyril nodded his agreement.

They sat in silence again. Amber came to them eventually and began to knead the blanket Sacha had swaddled her in when she was a vulnerable kitten. She almost looked like a full-grown cat now.

The ringing of Sacha's full-volume default ringtone filled the room, shattering the silence they found themselves in.

"Sacha? Are you there?"

It was Sacha's dad. Sacha's breath hitched in his throat. He was suddenly reminded of how close he was to going home. It felt far in the future, even if it was less than three hours away.

"Yes, Papa, I am. Are you in Syracuse?"

"Yes, we're almost out of the city. We got stuck in a jam."

Sacha chuckled a little. It all felt so surreal, like he was in a movie. He could hardly believe that he was going home.

"Sacha? What's the name of the person you're with? We want to be able to thank him when we get there."

"His name is Cyril. Cyril Galanos."

Cyril looked up at Sacha, looking a little confused.

"Okay. Thank you. You're, um, you're safe, really, right?"

Sacha smiled a bit into the phone. "Yes, I really am."

"Okay." His dad went quiet. "Okay," he added a little more forcefully. "We'll be there soon."

"Okay, Papa. I love you."

The line went quiet. "I love you, too." His voice was shaking. Then the beep came that indicated his dad had hung up.

Sacha looked at Cyril. "That was my dad. They're in Syracuse."

Cyril nodded. "Okay. Will they need food?"

Sacha nodded. "I doubt they're stopping to eat."

***

Sacha heard the car doors shut before he saw his mom.

When he saw her, he thought he was going to faint. All the blood rushed to his feet. His heart stopped beating for what felt like a minute. She was black-haired with hazel eyes, his same hazel eyes. People always said that they knew Sacha was his mother's son from those eyes of his.

His dad came out next. He was tall – something Sacha didn't inherit – but had the same black hair and green eyes. He was starting to bald and he had gray hairs that Sacha didn't remember. Luckily, his mom's side didn't bald.

Nothing could stop Sacha. He ran to the door, throwing it open, and ran into his mother's arms.

He saw the moment when she saw him, the recognition in her eyes. The shock, the awe, the happiness, the sadness for the years they lost together, all those painful moments and emotions overwhelmed her as she held her son.

It wasn't long before both of them were crying. She held Sacha tightly, pulling him close like she would never let him go.

"We missed you," she hiccuped a bit. "We missed you so much, Sacha. It's so good to see you again."

"I missed you. I thought about you and Papa every day."

She hugged him tighter at that. Eventually, Sacha's dad joined the hug, tears rolling down his face, too.

"We never thought we would see you again, Sacha," his dad said, holding both Sacha and his mother tight.

"I – I still can't believe I'm out."

"Yes, and now you're in my arms. You never have to go back. That much, I promise you," Sacha's mom whispered into his hair, rubbing it gently.

They were silent, hugging and crying and making up for the four years lost in precious, loving seconds.

"How did it happen? How did you get out?" his mother eventually asked, pushing Sacha back a bit so she could look at him.

"M – The man who kept me, he died of an infection. I was able to escape. He left my room unlocked."

His mother smiled and cupped his face, right below the scar Emery had left on his cheek. When Sacha looked into her face, it was as though she'd aged ten years in the four he'd been gone.

"So, a miracle. God was watching over you." She smiled warmly. "Your birthday is in two weeks. We'll be able to celebrate it together. You're even home for

Christmas. I never believed I would see another one of your birthdays or spend another Christmas with you."

Her face contorted with sadness as she started sobbing again, pulling Sacha close.

When all had calmed down and the stories and emotions of years had been passed silently through hugs, Cyril came from behind.

"Mrs. and Mr. Matisse, my name is Cyril Galanos. I found your son after he'd escaped. I'm a former doctor and I was able to help nurse him back to health."

Sacha's mom walked towards Cyril, smiling. "You're my son's guardian angel?"

Cyril took a moment of pause, then smiled a bit. "I guess you could say that."

Her eyes filled with emotion as she looked upon the long-haired, tattooed doctor. "I cannot put into words my thanks. You gave us our son back. I just ... you saved him. You're practically family for that. We will forever be in your debt."

A twinge of sadness flickered through Cyril's eyes as he smiled genuinely at Sacha's mom. "You don't owe me anything. It's okay."

"Please, allow us to have even one meal with you. I'll drive you to my home and pay for your plane ticket back."

"Well, I – um, I cooked you and your husband food. I didn't know if you'd eaten on your way here."

"No, no, you're too kind!"

Cyril smiled, opening the door to his cabin. "I insist. We can eat outside if it makes you more comfortable."

Sacha's mom moved towards the door when Sacha willingly went inside, patting Cyril's shoulder. The bond between the two men was obvious. This was not the man who'd hurt Sacha. And he had been hurt. She could see it in his eyes and the way he carried himself now.

Sacha's mom looked around, taking in the whole place. She noticed the handmade bed, the thick, warm bedsheets, the warm fireplace, the medical supplies, the glasses on Sacha's face, and the cat that wandered around the place. Sacha had been cared for – that much was obvious. His dad went straight to the table. Ever since an accident at his work, well, Sacha guessed it was five years ago, he had a bad knee that acted up if he stood for too long.

Cyril went into the kitchen and served the food. Amber came from around the bend to Cyril's bedroom to investigate the new people.

Sacha's mom laughed a bit. "Is the cat yours, Cyril?"

"No, she's all Sacha's. Sacha raised her."

"Well, then, I guess she's coming with us."

They all exchanged a laugh, then silence fell over them.

"Really, Cyril, if you think of anything we can do to repay you, let us know, okay?"

Cyril nodded, but looked pensive as he began to eat his soup. Sacha wondered what was on his mind and if, after tomorrow, he'd ever see Cyril again. The thought didn't sit well with him. How was he supposed to choose between his family and the man who'd saved him? His brother.

That's tomorrow's problem, Sacha.

Again, that little Cyril-voice in his head told him everything would be okay. Sacha just had to believe it.

Chapter 33

The car ride back to Hope was long. New York was never a big state in Cyril's head. He was from a small town not far outside Oswego – not far from the United States-Canada border, not far from Lake Ontario, and not too far from New York City. It was easy to forget the expanse that was New York State in that small town, in that small cabin.

Trees blended into one and the conversation between Sacha and his parents was hopeful. Sacha and Cyril had both said that they didn't really want to talk about what happened, so his family did the talking. They couldn't stop telling Sacha about everything he'd missed while he was gone, how happy they were to have him back. Soon, the conversation changed to what they wanted to do for his birthday. Cyril would chip in when asked or when he thought of something to say, but he mostly stayed quiet.

Finally, they arrived in Hope. The sun had started to set, but that was only natural – it was winter, after all. They'd driven through snow-covered trees in the Upstate.

Sacha's home wasn't big. In fact, it reminded Cyril of his cabin more than the houses he saw when he worked in Syracuse. It was a ranch with a dirty door and windows, but the garden in the front was netted – probably for the deer. Cyril recognized the tomato plants. It must've been a dormant vegetable garden.

Sacha's mother hurried to open the door to welcome the two of them in. "I'm sorry for the mess. We didn't really have time to clean," she said with a chuckle.

Cyril chuckled, too. The house was almost perfectly clean inside and smelled of vanilla. "It's okay. I understand."

Sacha's mother led them all to the living room, while Sacha's father brought over four bottles of craft beer.

He smiled at Sacha. "You're finally old enough to drink."

Sacha chuckled. Cyril thought over any medication that Sacha might be taking, but then remembered that Sacha wasn't taking anything more than acetaminophen and ibuprofen. He chuckled a little to himself, which drew a look from Sacha. Cyril was quick to wave his hand dismissively.

"I just remembered something."

Sacha nodded and accepted the beer from his father. The four of them toasted then all took a sip of their beers. Cyril hummed a little. He missed craft beer, all those years in the mountains.

After a little beat of happy, content silence, Sacha's mother spoke. "I'm headed to go make dinner." She looked at Cyril. "Don't you dare ask to help. This is for us to do for you."

Cyril laughed a little. "How'd you figure it out?"

"You just seem like the type," Sacha's mother said with a laugh.

Sacha and his father got talking about different things. Apparently the Buffalo Bills were getting a lot better recently. Cyril wouldn't know. He wasn't into sports. Yet to see Sacha's face light up and for him to talk, actually talk, excitedly without hesitation made Cyril smile widely.

However, after a while, a thought started to hang around in Cyril's head. One that bothered him and needed to get out.

He stood up politely and said he was going to talk to Sacha's mother. Clementine – if Cyril remembered correctly.

Cyril knocked a little on the doorframe. "Mrs. Matisse?"

Sacha's mother smiled and looked back at Cyril. She was chopping up yellow potatoes and garlic.

"You aren't asking to help, right?"

Cyril cracked a smile. "No, I'm not, Mrs. Matisse."

Sacha's mother waved her hand. "Call me Clementine."

"Clementine, then. I, um, pardon. I'm not the best at talking."

"Neither was Sacha. It ... it took him a long time to climb out of his shell."

Cyril swallowed a little. "I'm a doctor."

Suddenly, he had Clementine's attention. "Did he – ?"

Cyril shook his head. "I left medicine for personal reasons a few years ago. I found him half-dead in the forest near where I live. I know the house he came from, now, but I wanted you to know that the man who kept him captive is dead. He died of an infection. Sacha almost did, too, but I helped him."

Clementine's knife fell and she turned to look at him. In fact, she didn't just look at him, she came and hugged him.

"You, a total stranger, saved my son?" There were tears in her eyes. In the other room, the TV was turned to a football game and Sacha and his father were watching happily. "Even after you left medicine, you saved him?"

Cyril nodded. "I guess I did."

Clementine hugged him tighter. "Thank you. Thank you for being my son's guardian angel."

Gently, Cyril rubbed her back as she cried a little into him.

"Was it bad? The condition he was in?"

"It was bad, yes."

She went quiet again. "Thank you. Thank you so much. I will never be able to repay you, but thank you. Know that if you need anything, you can come to me."

Cyril took a breath. "About that, I had a question."

"Anything," Clementine breathed.

"I'd like to come practice here," Cyril blurted. He took a moment in the silence that followed to put his thoughts together. "I know you hardly know me, but I wanted to ask your permission. Sacha would say yes no matter what, but that doesn't mean I'm wanted, you know?" He took a breath. "I can't imagine living away from him anymore. He's become like a little brother to me. I took care of him. I helped him break out of his shell and ... " *Made him ready to live in society again.*

Clementine nodded her understanding, taking a step back with a warm smile that created peaks and valleys on her face. "We would love to have you. It's a long drive to the nearest doctor out here."

Cyril's heart sang. "Are you sure?"

Clementine laughed. "Just make sure you get vetted as a Medicaid provider. There's a lot of people out here on Medicaid and the nearest doctor doesn't even take it."

Cyril nodded, smiling. He'd intended to, anyway. "Thank you. I cannot put into words how much I owe you for that."

"We owe you more, I guarantee that. I just have to ask, don't you have any family or anything? Anyone who would miss you up there?"

Cyril shook his head, looking a little sad. "I was a foster kid, never adopted. Didn't really get to know many people. My only real friend died maybe five years ago."

"I'm so sorry." Clementine gave him a kind look. "You can stay with us until you're set up."

"Thank you."

"No, thank you." Clementine laughed a little. "Go with the other boys and watch some football. Even if you don't like it."

Cyril laughed a little. "Never did."

Clementine laughed heartily. "I never did either."

***

One month after Sacha's homecoming ...

Each breath that Sacha breathed let out a puff of white steam into the air. The Lake was just starting to ice over as Cyril and Sacha sat on the dock, feet hanging off the edge, looking out onto the water. They'd cleared a small area for themselves and brought two cushions.

The sky was dark and filled with stars. So far out from the city, you might even see the Milky Way if the night allowed. It was getting late and Sacha was getting tired, but he wanted to stay up until midnight to open their presents. It was a long-standing tradition in his family for Christmas.

"Sacha," Cyril began, turning to look at him. The two had hot chocolate warming their hands through their gloves. The winds were always cold on the Lake.

"Yeah?"

"This is the first Christmas I'm celebrating since Oliver died. I ... um, I used to celebrate with his family, but his family stopped wanting to see me after he died."

Sacha nodded quietly. "I'm sorry."

"It is what it is."

A beat of silence passed between them. Eventually, after an awkwardly long silence, Cyril spoke. "I'm really glad that I found you, Sacha. You're my family now. Your family has been wonderful to me. Even standing up for me when the cops came to check me out."

Both of them knew what Cyril was referring to. When news surfaced that the long-missing Sacha Matisse had returned home, the FBI had come to investigate. Upon looking at Emery Abberton's mansion, they found the bodies of three other victims, victims like Sacha. Sacha was his sole survivor.

Emery's mother had been covering for him and spilled the whole truth. After that and a quick investigation into Cyril's connections, Cyril's name had been cleared, in part because of the way that Sacha's family stood up for him.

"I never imagined that I'd get out alive."

Cyril patted him on the back. "None of that matters now. You're a survivor. Now, you're home."

Sacha laughed a little. "I just don't know what the hell I'm going to do now."

Cyril got serious. "Study. Learn something. There's got to be a community college close to here."

"But what would I study?"

Cyril shrugged. "I don't know. That's up to you. You could become a therapist, a social worker. I can see you as a woodworker."

The two of them sat in silence for a little while longer. "I was thinking about marine health. Something like environmental science but for the lakes."

Cyril smiled and laughed. "That suits you. I don't know why I didn't think of that before."

Sacha laughed a little, too. "I guess it does."

Sacha's phone began to buzz in his pocket. He always kept it on do not disturb except for certain family members, one of which was his mother.

Sacha picked up his phone, only to see the time was 11:55 p.m.

"Where are you two?" Sacha's mom sounded panicked, afraid almost. Sacha and Cyril had simply lost track of time, but Sacha was sure that it reminded her all too much of the night that her son disappeared.

"It's okay, Maman. We're at the dock. We'll be there soon."

Sacha's mom took a deep breath. "Okay. Okay. We'll see you soon."

It was a ten-minute walk back to Sacha's house from the dock, but once they got inside, they were hit with warmth and the twinkling of the Christmas tree.

Sacha's mom was smiling warmly at the both of them. "Sacha, Cyril, we want you to open your presents first."

Sacha smiled and nudged Cyril, who was a little in shock.

Sacha's father handed Sacha and Cyril each a box. They motioned for Cyril and Sacha to open it at the same time, which they obliged. Inside, there were matching carved goldfish made from wood, hand-finished and painted. Each one was almost the same, except for those little details that hand-finishing made.

Sacha's mom was the one that spoke to Sacha first. "We wanted to welcome you both into the family. Sacha, we're welcoming you back. We want you to know that we'll always love you, no matter what. Okay? We're just happy to have you home."

"And Cyril," Sacha's father said next, not giving Sacha even a moment to absorb what had been said, "the goldfish is a symbol of our family. We wanted you to have one that matched Sacha's. You're a part of this family now. You saved our first son. If ever you need a place to go, we'll always be here for you. Regardless. Okay?"

Cyril bit his lip, tears forming in his eyes. Though Sacha had heard the speech about loving him unconditionally many times over the past month, Cyril was being welcomed for the first time. Cyril nodded a bit, struggling to absorb the information.

"Th – " His voice broke a bit. "Thank you. This means so much to me. Thank you."

Sacha's mom looked upon Cyril with kind eyes. "Of course. You're always welcome here."

Cyril nodded, but the disbelief was palpable.

"Let's move on to your other presents."

For Cyril – all new gardening tools, scented lotion for his hands, and an invitation to work on the garden in front of Sacha's house. Again, Cyril was emotional. After all, now he had two gardens – Sacha's and his own.

For Sacha – a new, thick blanket and bedsheets for his room, a Buffalo Bills jersey, signed by a star player that even Sacha didn't recognize but knew was important from his father's pride, and a new cat tower for Amber.

Sacha didn't have money to buy his mom and dad gifts, but Cyril had given them each $100 in cash, explaining that he didn't know them well enough to buy them presents quite yet.

The two understood. Of course they did.

As the night wound down and the tiredness set in, Cyril went to the guest room and Sacha went to his bedroom that hadn't changed much since he'd disappeared.

Lying there, Sacha felt warm and loved in a way he hadn't before. His mind went to Emery, but he quickly thought of the goldfish, of Cyril, of his parents, and of the content feeling that now rested in his chest. The image of Emery didn't belong there anymore.

Sacha didn't just own himself.

He was his own person now, with a brother and parents. He was happy. But, most importantly, Sacha was at peace.

That peace was worth more than gold and tasted sweeter than any nectar from the heavens.

Acknowledgements

I'd like to acknowledge everyone who helped encourage me and bring this story to life — I couldn't have completed this one without your help.

About the Author

Harper is a long-time writer turned whump enthusiast. She enjoys a variety of different types of whump and likes to not leave any genre unturned. She has a love for fantasy and combines intricate soft worldbuilding with hurt to create stories that explore the human and nonhuman condition. She also has a love for surrealism. Though a private person, Harper incorporates parts of her life in her stories to create pieces that she hopes are both comforting and difficult to read at times.

www.ingramcontent.com/pod-product-compliance
Lightning Source LLC
LaVergne TN
LVHW091142080826
845145LV00008B/2227

* 9 7 8 1 9 5 9 3 3 0 4 7 9 *